Marguerite O'Callaghan was born in Cork City in 1982, and now lives in North London with artist Luci Maclaren and a black cat called Angelo. She is a self-confessed ethical hedonist, existentialist, animal lover, and she claims to laugh more than the average person. Marguerite also works as a television producer, specialising in true crime. She has a degree in English and Sociology, an MA in Irish Writing, and has studied Creative Writing at the University of East Anglia at post-graduate level.

Also by Marguerite O'Callaghan

Fiction
This Dark Town I: When You're Gone
This Dark Town III: Us and Them

Poetry
The Silent Field

This Dark Town II:

THE HOUSE IN THE WOODS

marguerite o'callaghan

ISBN-13: 978-1977530318
ISBN-10: 1977530311

for lonely girls, everywhere.

1

A GENTLE MIST rests over the land surrounding the big old farmhouse, and the sheep start to huddle together at one end of the sloping fields. The thick woods at the front of the house are making their own sounds now; branches are creaking, and leaves seem to whisper. In the daylight, these woods allow a certain amount of light in, and are certainly not scary. A few of the children from the local village of Southam have started to come here at weekends, and they ride their bikes to the edge of the woods to climb trees, play hide-and-seek, or build forts. But they know not to go past the woods towards the house at the top. That's where Melvin Todd and his wife live, and they have two big dogs, and a large gate with a sign that says: 'No Trespassing!'.

This evening, Melvin is gazing out of the large window of the front room, past the rose garden, and the long tree-lined driveway, to the security gate at the bottom. His right hand is holding his favourite blue and white striped mug, and he shifts his weight back and forth, until he's almost rolling on his feet, occasionally taking a gulp of tea without looking down at the mug. His eyes are still, almost glazed over, and his mind begins to wander past the village of Southam, the woods, and farm lands that surround it, past all the sounds of the English countryside. In fact, he's not only somewhere else in his mind, but in a completely different period of time: Texas, in the seventies.

He misses how huge America is; how vast and full of possibility the world seems when you can drive for two hours, and barely pass another vehicle. There's nowhere here that Melvin can do that; not in the middle of the Northamptonshire countryside. He misses the Texas heat, too. In the years since they moved here, his skin has gone a pasty white, and he has developed eczema on his elbows and the back of his neck. He's adjusted to most other things though, and even started to enjoy British customs, culture and people, and finds it easier to blend in than he thought he would. Christine seems to be doing fine too, and people probably think any strangeness, or difference they sense when they are around the couple, is down to the fact they are American, and have been brought up in the middle of nowhere. When Christine doesn't understand a joke, or fails to bond with the other women in the village, they probably think she is just shy on account of her sheltered and religious upbringing, and that suits Melvin just fine. This way, people give them a wide berth, and they don't have problems with any nosy neighbours, or people wanting to come to the house. That would have ruined everything.

Melvin snaps out of his trance when he hears the phone ringing. Christine has heard it too, and runs downstairs, but her husband is standing in front of the phone by the time she reaches it, and he shakes his head at her.

'There's no point in answering, is there? I'm not expecting anyone at this hour, and they can leave a message if it's important.'

Christine nods briefly in understanding, and when

the ringing has stopped, she offers him another cup of tea. Melvin declines.

'Have you fed her yet?' he asks.

'No, but she can have those potatoes and fish left over from lunch. Unless you want them, do you?'

Christine is taken aback by her husband's consideration. She tells him that she's perfectly happy not to have the potatoes and fish, and makes her way to the kitchen to put them into the plastic container they use to feed the girl. Christine hums to herself, and cracks a little smile as she dishes out the food. Melvin is in such a good mood today and seems serene and gentle. She had grown used to his tantrums over the years, as well as the distance she feels from him now. Most of the time he barely looks at her, hardly ever addressed her needs directly, and any kindness is an afterthought, following an episode when he's hit her, or ignored her for days. But something is changing. Maybe they are close to the change they had been waiting for, she thinks to herself.

A few minutes later, Melvin joins Christine in the kitchen and takes a look at the plastic container with the food inside. Christine looks at him, waiting for the explanation as to what she's done wrong. Instead, he smiles.

'Let's give her some of that new cheese too... and maybe a bit of fruit... Are there any bananas left?'

Christine nods at his words, and immediately walks to the fridge, takes the cheese to the chopping board and starts to cut a generous chunk. Melvin saunters over casually, with a slight smile on his face. Feeling his presence, she looks up for a second, then puts the cheese back in fridge, and takes a banana and pear from the fruit bowl on the counter behind her. Melvin's behaviour is unnerving, and she hopes he will stop. He hasn't looked at her like this in years; since they used to sleep together.

'Christine?'

His voice is loud and makes the hairs on the back of her neck stand on edge. But acting scared is something Christine knows he finds offensive, so she looks at him bravely, instead.

'Yes. What is it Melvin?'

'Aren't you wondering why we need to give her this extra food?'

He moves closer, and Christine can feel her heart start to race and a heavy panic move from her stomach to her chest, like his hands are already on her, about to choke her. She can also feel that her face has started to flush pink, and there's a stirring in that part of her mind that never stops; the part that's now furiously trying to figure out what she's done wrong this time. What could it be that's making her husband mad? There has to be something she's forgotten, something she said, or didn't say... or maybe she hadn't cleaned the top-floor shower room properly this morning. Melvin reaches out and grabs her arm gently, turning her to face him fully. Christine winces.

'It's happening.'

She stares blankly at Melvin, and has no idea what he means. Then it occurs to her; he must mean the girl. Christine's heart soars, then sinks, then soars again. This could be the best, or the worst thing to ever happen to her.

'You mean... sh-she's pregnant?'

Melvin nods his head, beams at her, then pulls her close so her head rests reluctantly on his chest. Christine hasn't been this close to anyone for a long time, and she is somewhat comforted, yet longs for him to let her go, at the same time.

'You know what this means, don't you? This child is going to change everything, Christine. Not just for you and me, but for all mankind... for the whole planet... maybe even the universe!'

He starts to pace up and down the room, and clasps his hands excitedly.

'I... We have been waiting for this for so long, haven't we? I mean, this is basically why I was put on this earth Christine; to father this child. It's my seed that will make the next messiah, and you are going to help me. Obviously, you won't be the biological mother, but I don't think that matters. This girl is unclean. She's broken, Christine, and although she's from the right bloodline, as soon as she has the child we won't need her anymore. We can live as a family. We can sit back and watch as my son, as our son Christine, saves the world!'

Christine is pacing now too, and biting at her nails. Her whole body is full of excitement. Melvin has been waiting for over thirty years to have this son. It was a prophecy that their whole community was built on back on the ranch in Texas, and was backed up by the priests there, as well as Melvin's own father, Joseph Todd. His vision was that his first son would have a son with a beautiful young woman with long black hair. His father had written prayers, songs, and drawn pictures of this woman, and when a new family, the Pernots, moved to the ranch in the early nineties, it was obvious to everyone, that sixteen-year-old Margaret Pernot was the one they had been waiting for.

It's been five months since Kate Stone went missing,

and five months since she's seen anyone, besides Melvin and Christine. She assumes that her family, and everyone, thinks she's dead at this stage. But the reality is that being alive has been much worse than death for her.

Melvin raped her for the first time, about three weeks after she got here, when he'd decided she had passed some sort of test, after nearly starving to death. He informed her that they had to make a baby together, and pretty much every night since then, he has come down into the basement and forced himself on her. Kate never resisted. She didn't see the point, and had learned to disappear somewhere when he was on top of her, and to replace his grunting sounds with the rhythm of a song in her head, or think about running through forests and across fields. Kate escaped in her mind every single night, and as the weeks and months went by, she felt herself slipping further and further away. She wasn't Kate Stone anymore. She was someone, something else; a creature maybe, who didn't speak, who ran and ran, and screeched like the howling wind, until it reached freedom, wherever that might be. Kate longed for the vast ocean, for salty air, the smell of nature that was growing, crawling, and never stopping. Her family and friends seemed small and insignificant in comparison to what she yearned for now: death, an ending, and peace.

Before that first night that Melvin stripped her naked, Kate had never been mistreated by a man. She'd had her bum grabbed a few times in night clubs, and men looked at her constantly, of course. Kate was a successful model, conventionally beautiful, used to people staring at her, boys wanting her, and girls wanting to be her. But the way she was treated by

Melvin, was something she never imagined could happen to anyone. She couldn't get her head around how calmly and assuredly this man could take from her, piece by piece; unravelling her like he was peeling an onion. He looked at her, touched her, and she felt herself slipping away, like she was drowning slowly and peacefully in a small pond. His mouth, his hands, the taste of him... it all faded in just a matter of weeks, until Kate was sure she'd gone deaf, or her brain had stopped working. Because, when he was with her everything was slow, distant, and heavy. Her body was there in the basement, but the rest of her was not connected to it, and she wondered if she would ever feel anything again. Lying there in the dark, when he left, she wondered about all the times she had seen sexual violence mentioned in newspapers, or heard about women coming forward to say that a friend of the family, or their mum's boyfriend had molested them when they were children. They said it affected their whole lives, indefinitely, forever, and she remembers not being able to imagine what they meant by that. Now, she did. Melvin wasn't even violent with her really. He was rough, disgusting, and wanted to do the most perverted things to her, but he didn't beat her, and he didn't torture her. Still, Kate longs for death, every single day. She wants it more than she wants to go home to her family, and to her, the world she knows and loves, will never be a place that she belongs again.

2

Lydia Stone hasn't seen her mother Barbara since the night she packed a suitcase and left them two weeks ago. But, she has agreed to meet her for a coffee today in the village. There's a chill in the air, and Lydia buttons up her tan-coloured, woollen pea coat to the top, and adjusts her green beanie so it's snug on her head and covering her ears fully. She walks slowly and mindfully up Well Walk, passed her favourite local pub, The Wells Tavern, passed the museum, and the little primary school that she and Kate used to go to. The streets are quiet today, and Lydia only sees a couple of people until she reaches Flask Walk, and turns on to Hampstead High Street. It's always busier there. She rounds the corner right by the underground station and a crowd of people, fresh off the train, seem to storm towards her. Lydia feels anxiety rising in her chest. Her breath quickens, her palms start to sweat, and that familiar tingling begins in her face. She's had panic attacks almost daily for the past month, and is completely exhausted from them. Today, she wants to be strong, so she can have a proper conversation with her mother, and ask the questions she needs to. She does not want to have a panic attack on the street either, for that matter.

Lydia takes a deep breath, waits for the pedestrian crossing light to flash green. When it does, she jogs across the road, and straight up the little hill towards The Holly Bush where she's meeting her mum.

'Shake it off Lydia' she whispers to herself.

'You've got this.'

She's surprised to see her mother sitting outside when she gets there. Barbara's wearing large sunglasses and a winter parka with a fur hood. Lydia can't help but smile when she sees her. Mother and daughter embrace, and Barbara removes her sunglasses with one hand as she hugs Lydia tightly with the other.

'Let me look at you. My goodness Lydia, you are so bloody beautiful. I've missed you so much, darling.'

Lydia smiles at Barbara and suggests they go inside and find a table. They take a seat by the window, a young waiter arrives quickly with menus, and takes their drinks order. Barbara asks for a glass of Chardonnay, although it's not like her to drink in the day, and Lydia decides to join her.

'Maybe alcohol will actually help with my anxiety!' she says with a smile, as the waiter goes off to get their drinks.

'Are you still not sleeping? Still the panic? You were doing alright for a while, weren't you?'

A few months back, Lydia had pretended she was feeling better because she'd started becoming paranoid her mental health problems were making the situation between her parents worse. So, she feigned recovery and concealed her dark circles and pale, blotchy skin with some very effective make-up. Part of her knew that she wasn't really to blame, and it was the fact that her sister was missing and presumed dead, that was tearing the family apart. But maybe, just maybe, if she was stronger, they could be too, she thought. When Kate disappeared back in May, a black hole had appeared in the family, and although the three of them loved each other very much, Lydia and her parents had grown apart, and the space that Kate left when she disappeared had become bigger and bigger as the months went by. The shock, grief, and anger had made all three of them retreat from the once loving and peaceful home they had together. They say you have to come together as a family when something tragic like this happens, and that's the only way you will gain strength. But all Lydia had seen and felt was loneliness and darkness in their once warm and loving home. Every time she saw her parents, Lydia saw the sadness in their eyes, and she was sure that every time they looked at her, Kate's identical twin, they could only think about their missing child. Lydia felt invisible now. She'd lost her sister, kind of lost her parents, and she held the grief and love for Kate close to her. For now, her love for her twin was completely intertwined with the grief of losing her. She couldn't feel one without the other, and there was no peace to be found in that.

By the time Barbara and Lydia have finished their soup and sandwiches, Lydia plucks up the courage to ask her mum what she has been longing to. She clears her throat, sits up in her chair, then sits back again, and fiddles with her napkin. Barbara notices, and leans forward with her elbows on the table.

'What is it, darling?' she asks gently.

Lydia looks up at her mother and takes a breath.

'Dad and you. You were fighting a while back about something and I... well, he won't tell me what it is, and I really want to know, Mum.'

'I'm not sure what to say to that.'

Barbara sits back, and looks over her right shoulder, out of the window. Lydia's eyes drop to the table; she will have to be more forceful. She'd practised what she was going to say in the mirror at home, but now that her mum was right in front of her, it's so difficult.

'Mum, if you don't tell me what's going on, then we will not be able to have a relationship in the future. I know you and Dad were arguing about something from the past that you hid from us. I don't know what he found out or what he suspects, but I do know that it has a lot to do with why you left.'

Barbara is still looking out of the window and hasn't acknowledged what Lydia is saying.

'Mum? Are you just going to ignore me?'

Still, her mother doesn't look at Lydia, but there's tears in her eyes. Lydia grabs her coat and bag.

'I'm serious. You can stay out of my life completely if you don't talk to me.'

Barbara turns to look at Lydia.

'You don't mean that, do you?'

'Are you going to tell me what this secret is from your past? Are you going to tell me why Dad stopped trusting you?'

Barbara's eyes drop for a second, and when she looks at Lydia tears are streaming down her face. Lydia's face doesn't soften.

'Last chance, Mum...?'

Lydia shakes her head in disappointment and anger.

'You've already lost one daughter, and now you're going to lose another. I don't believe this!'

Lydia turns and walks out of the pub. Barbara watches as she passes the window; her hands are shaking, she can barely contain a sob, and covers her mouth to try to stop herself. The young waiter comes over to ask if she's okay. Barbara didn't realise it earlier, but she recognises him, and wonders if he knows her daughters. Almost on cue, he tells her how sorry he is about Kate.

'I can't imagine what you and your family are going through, Mrs Stone. I'm so sorry. The manager said that your lunch today is complimentary.'

Barbara can barely manage a 'thank you' and simply nods and smiles at him through the tears. She's grateful she doesn't have to stay and fuss over the bill, and goes to the toilets to splash some cold water on her face before leaving. When she steps back out into the day, she is grateful for her large sunglasses too; her eyes are still burning with tears as she makes her way back to her rented flat at the top of the hill. She was hoping that Lydia would come and take a look at it with her after lunch, and maybe even help to choose some cushions and throws for the living room. But the day isn't going the way she imagined. There are some things she can't tell her daughter. She doesn't want to hurt, or scare her. Lydia has enough on her plate with anxiety and panic attacks for God's sake, and finding out about her mother's past is not something that will help her right now.

Lydia can't face going home. She needs to walk, drink more, or talk to someone. She pulls her phone from her pocket and makes a call.

'It's me. She didn't say anything.'

'Baby, I'm sorry. Are you able to meet?'

'Yes please. Our secret place?'

'Perfect, I can be there in twenty?'

'Okay. See you soon. Love you.'

If her mother can keep secrets, Lydia can too.

3

Jared Cooper is working on another sex-trafficking case, and liaising with Detective Thomas McCarthy again. Since Kate Stone went missing in May, the pair have worked together a few times, and grown to be on pretty friendly terms, although the Kate Stone case is no longer active.

Jared pops his head around the open door of McCarthy's office.

'We good? I've got to be somewhere, so unless there's anything else...'

McCarthy looks tired, and yawns as he shakes his head.

'Nope. I'll email you those documents now, and I suppose we can talk again in a few days, unless you find something out about these Russian girls.'

'Cool. Have a good one, mate!'

McCarthy raises his hand in a casual wave, and watches as Jared walks awkwardly down the hall. He is so square, polite, and American, it makes McCarthy chuckle. Even the way Jared says 'cool' and 'mate' seems wrong; kind of like hearing a nun swearing. McCarthy has always imagined that Jared would be more suited to a career as a missionary, or school counsellor, not a sex crimes expert who sometimes works undercover. It's so unbelievable, it actually works. No-one would ever guess what Jared is really trying to do; break into the UK's sex trafficking scene from the inside, and find missing girls who've been forced to work as prostitutes. If this earnest, clean-living, square thing is an act, it certainly works. Jared is just the kind of guy you just trust completely and implicitly, and as far as McCarthy knows, he has no bad habits, no secret past, and he isn't running from anything. He's just a guy who's passionate about a certain area of crime.

4

Lydia sits under the beer garden's gazebo, smoking a cigarette. On the table in front of her are two pints of beer. Her black hood is up, and she's wearing sunglasses; she doesn't want anyone to recognise her, not just because of who she's meeting, but she can't bear the thought of anyone recognising her, looking at her with pity, or someone mentioning Kate. Her mother's refusal to speak to her has really made Lydia angry too, and she just wants to get drunk. She hears a familiar voice call her name, and for a moment she thinks she's been busted. But when she sees who it is, she stands up, removes her glasses, and opens her arms for a hug. Jared hugs her so tightly, that Lydia's feet lift off the ground.

'Oh my god, I've missed you.'

Lydia is beaming from ear to ear. When she's around Jared, she feels hopeful and happy again. He sees something in her that no-one else does, and he's the kindest person she's ever met. The problem is that Jared's job would be in danger if anyone knew they were romantically involved, and although they've kissed and gone on seven or eight secret dates, things haven't progressed from there. Lydia knows that it's only been five weeks since they got together, but she feels like she's in love. The first time they saw one another was at Haven, when Lydia went looking for anyone who might know her sister. That night had been an eye-opening experience for her, to say the least; she'd kissed a girl, visited an S&M dungeon, and seen all sorts of wild fetish acts. She remembers seeing Jared at the bar at one point during the night, and again just before she left. She'd turned away for a second, and then thought that maybe he was looking at her because he knew or recognised Kate. But, when she turned back, he was gone. And that was that, until a couple of months later, Lydia saw him again outside the police station in Hendon, and she just freaked out. In that moment, she was convinced that Jared had something to do with Kate's disappearance. He had been in his car outside the station, about to drive to a meeting, but got out when he saw Lydia. She was completely manic; shouting and pointing at him, and it was another ten minutes before she believed that he was at the club that night in May because he was working on Kate's case too. They talked, Lydia cried, and Jared texted his colleague to say he was going to be late to the meeting. Then, he listened as she opened up about her sister, her own mental health, and fears about her family. He was instantly enthralled with her; she was the most beautiful girl he had ever seen, never mind been around, and she seemed to like talking to him. They ended up getting a cup of tea in a cafe down the road, and talking for the next hour. She asked him to stay in touch with her and wanted his number. Jared never really worked with people like that; he was more of a background kind of guy, working undercover, and he didn't really know what the protocol was in this situation. He guessed that he should have refused his personal number, but he wanted Lydia to have it. He also really wanted to see her again. That night, Lydia lay awake and couldn't stop thinking about him; she wondered if the feeling would wear off by morning, but the next day it was even stronger, and she texted, asking to meet, saying she needed some confidential advice. Lydia didn't have a plan. She didn't need advice. All she knew was that she had to see Jared soon, to see if what she felt was real. Two days later, he walked into a pizzeria in Camden to meet her, and every single cell in Lydia's body came alive. Their eyes met, and they could barely take them off one another for the rest of the night. Lydia knew she was in love for the first time, and Jared felt it too. He actually hadn't stopped thinking about her since that night at Haven all those months ago, and he scolded himself that he could think about someone who was going through a tragedy in such a way. He had never done something as daring as this. He'd had a couple of relationships back home in Upstate New York, but since he'd been in the UK for the past few years, he hadn't met anyone he liked enough to go beyond a second or third date. Plus, he was kind of married to the job. That night in Camden, he told Lydia that he was going to be thirty in a few days and instead of running away in shock at how old he was, she had begged him to let her celebrate with him. She reached out and held his hand in hers, leaned in close, and told him that she never believed in love at first sight, until now.

'All I did was see you, and you never left my mind. I thought it was because I was paranoid that you knew Kate, but that wasn't it. My heart knew you, Jared. I'm sorry if that sounds too intense. You don't know me, but I... I don't feel like this, usually. I mean, I've been numb and lost since Kate went... actually, if I'm honest, I've been lost for years...'

Jared listened intently and squeezed her hand back. This was something, and he knew it. He had to see her again.

Today, in the beer garden is another meeting that they had to have in secret. Jared longs to take Lydia to the cinema, or walk hand-in-hand with her down the Southbank, or even go somewhere decent for dinner, like a legitimate couple. But they have to meet in empty, cold beer gardens, bad Chinese restaurants, or grotty old pubs, instead.

'Take me away for the weekend?' she says suddenly.

Lydia's eyes are shining, and her heart is racing. She is desperate to spend some time alone with Jared; to kiss him, undress for him, make love to him, wake up next to him, and breathe in his morning smell. She's fantasised so many times about a future with this man, but for starters, a romantic weekend in the Cotswolds will do nicely.

'Imagine it: champagne in bed, room service, walks in the countryside. There are some really nice spa hotels...'

Jared smiles, and nods his head slowly. How can he say no to this girl?

'Can we? Seriously?'

Lydia is almost squealing.

'Oh my god, when? I can go this weekend, can you?'

Jared stops smiling.

'Hang on. Hang on, okay? I need to sort some things out, and I definitely can't this weekend.'

Lydia's face drops in disappointment, and she looks away. It's not like her to be stroppy, but she wants this weekend away more than anything.'

'I promise I will take you away to a beautiful hotel and it'll be perfect, and you can have as much champagne and room service as your heart desires, Lydia Stone.'

His sweet talking has worked, and Lydia is smiling

again.

'I like it when you call me that, Jared Cooper.'

5

Kate isn't expecting to see Melvin or Christine until this evening. She's already had her morning meal, and they've emptied the toilet bucket too. Her stomach turns, almost in synchronicity with the turn of the key in the lock. Melvin sometimes does this when the mood takes him; comes down here in the middle of the day to have his way with her. But he seems different today, and when he comes in, he greets her with a tone that's almost enthusiastic. Maybe he doesn't want sex, Kate thinks to herself.

'Hello there!'

'Hi Melvin'

Kate is surprised at just how flat and monosyllabic her voice sounds. But she can't help herself; he sickens her. She notices he's carrying a small paper bag, and as he sits next to her on the mattress, he hands it to her, and tells her to open it. Inside, is a pregnancy test.

'You know what to do with that, right?'

Kate looks from the box to Melvin, and back again. She nods and stares at it

'You haven't bled in a while, have you?'

Kate had missed most of her periods since she was captured, and assumed that the conditions in the basement, lack of daylight, and poor nutrition mean that there is no way she could conceive. If Melvin is right, and she is carrying a baby, his baby, things would maybe change around here. This is why he took her in the first place. He said she 'owed' him a child, and the baby was going to be the next messiah, and save the world. He unties her hands, and tells her to urinate on the stick so he can see what she's doing, and Kate gets up to go to the bucket. When she's done, she hands the stick back to him. Kate tilts her head to read the instructions on the side of the box.

'We have to wait, see if lines appear.' she tells him. As they wait, Kate realises for the first time what it would mean for her to be pregnant. Melvin had told her about the prophecy his father had on the ranch, all those years ago, and how it was Kate's own mother that was believed to be the one that would give birth to the new leader. Kate had spent many hours wondering how her mother had hidden this from everyone for over two decades, and how she escaped from Melvin and the others. All Kate had known when she was growing up, was that Barbara had a religious upbringing in the States, and her family moved around a lot. She said that her parents had died when she was a teenager, and she and her sister Jane went their separate ways, and led very different lives after that. Kate had seen photographs of her mum from the eighties, and she looked happy. Now, Kate knew that she was most likely involved in some sort of cult at that time, and was obviously a prisoner there. Kate sees her mother as a different person now; almost a stranger. Kate feels like she has no idea who her mum really is, and where she has really come from. It's also strangely comforting. Her mother knew Melvin, had probably been held captive by him and his father all those years ago, and now Kate is going through something similar. It gave her a strange hope that there could be a life after this, and perhaps she could use this pregnancy as a way to prove to Melvin she is not like her mother. It might also mean she would have more freedom, food, and comfort.

'What does that mean?' Melvin asks, when the two pink lines appear.

'Is that? Are you pregnant, or not?'

Melvin is on his feet, and staring expectantly at Kate. She picks up the stick and examines it for a few seconds.

'Yes. I'm pregnant, yes!'

She can hardly believe it, but she is actually happy, and can feel a smile on her face for the first time in five months. Kate's mind immediately begins to envisage the baby growing inside of her, and she places one hand on her stomach. It actually feels like she is slightly swollen already. That must mean she was at least a couple of months into the pregnancy, surely? How did she not notice this? Melvin is talking quickly and excitedly. He walks up the three steps to the basement door entrance, and shouts out for Christine to come quickly. He never leaves that door open, and in the thirty or forty seconds that it takes for Christine to get there, Kate enjoys a glimpse of natural light and clean air. Christine arrives out of breath.

'Sorry Melvin, I was changing the bed sheets.'

'Don't worry about that now, Christine. We have some news! The girl is pregnant, like I thought, with MY child, and you know what this means, don't you?'

Christine looks amazed. Her mouth hangs open in surprise, and she looks at Kate and smiles. Then, she makes her way to her, kneels down, and places one hand gently on Kate's stomach, then strokes her cheek gently.

'You clever, clever girl. This is what we brought you here for, and now you've gone and done it!'

Kate did not expect this. How could these two monsters change their attitudes so quickly? They kidnapped her, raped her, barely fed her, allowed her to fester in her own excrement for months, and now they decide to treat her with respect because she has something inside of her, they think is theirs? Melvin has started rambling again, and is talking about moving Kate into the house when it's been secured properly. Christine chimes in that she'll make sure there are fresh vegetables and fruit every day, and will pick up some vitamins from the pharmacy this afternoon. The couple are nodding, smiling, and at times clapping their hands in excitement, as Kate looks at them. Then, Melvin stops speaking, and turns to her. His face changes, and his brow becomes furrowed.

'Your life of sin. We must not forget that. You need to repent, and promise never to return to it. You belong to God, and the rest of your life must be dedicated to him. You, a sinful prostitute, have been granted this gift, even in light of all that you have done. You will give birth to the most holy, most divine soul. Now, bow your head!'

Kate doesn't even flinch, and although Melvin's voice is terrifying, she bows her head and joins her hands in prayer. If they need to believe she's the next Virgin Mary, she'll do her damn best to play the part. This new life inside of her could be her ticket to freedom. Melvin and Christine start whispering again about shopping and blankets, or something similar, and Kate watches them for a moment, but her eyes are quickly drawn to the open basement door behind them, and the daylight beyond it. In the distance, she can hear birdsong, and she knows there will be a way out

6

'Forgive me father for I have sinned. It has been... many, many years since my last confession.'

Barbara doesn't know who else to turn to. She has driven all the way to Mill Hill, to an old catholic church, and hopes that she won't see anyone she knows here.

'Father, I have lied to my family, to everyone, all of my life. I'm not the wife, or the mother I pretend to be. I've done some terrible things. The worst type of sins, Father.'

'My child, tell me what your sins are. That is the only way you can have forgiveness.'

Barbara is crying, and the priest bows his head, allowing her a moment to compose herself. She wipes her face and takes a breath. He continues:

'Our loving father forgives all. Remember that. But you must come to him with an open heart, and acknowledge what you have done.'

Barbara's mind flashes to a time she has longed to forget: the day at the quarry. Barbara is sixteen years old. The light is blinding, her throat is dry, she hasn't slept in days, and she's almost forgotten her own name. Her legs are heavy, and a strange pain runs down the right side of her body; from her pelvis to her knee. She has an infection after being raped repeatedly for about a week. Now that her father is dead and her mother is ill, there's no-one to protect her. The little girl next to her has gone mad. She's several years younger than Barbara, probably only twelve or thirteen, and she's wearing a faded blue cotton blouse, but her bottom half is completely naked. Her hair has been chopped off or pulled out in places, and her scalp is bald and bloody.

Both of her eyes are swollen and purple, her face smeared with dirt, and her lips dry and caked in blood. She's moaning, pulling at Barbara's skirt, and trying to grab her; the tiny slits of her eyes show a desperate soul, begging for help. Barbara thinks the girl has probably been passed around for several weeks. It's so shocking to see that Barbara cannot bear to look at her. She's powerless to help anyway. The girl's cries are growing more and more awful; guttural and low, like they are coming from a creature of some kind. Suddenly, one of the larger men from the group pulls Barbara and the girl close to the edge of the quarry by the scruff of their necks. Barbara is paralysed with fear, and tries to move as little as possible, although she's struggling to breathe. The man tells them both to look down at the other girls who ended up in the pit at the bottom, and Barbara can make out what looks like a few bodies. But it's hard to see that far down, and the dust and dizziness could be playing tricks with her eyes. Then the man leans down to say something into her ear. She trembles, sure that he is about to fling her over the edge any second. Instead he says:

'If you push her, we will let you live, Margaret. If you don't, then you both go over. Understand? That's the deal.'

Barbara can remember the moment when the girl realised what the man had said, and looked right at her. A second later, the man let go of them, Barbara grabbed the girl, and pushed her over as hard as she could. She was light as a feather, and didn't resist or scream, even on the way down. But, right after she heard her hit the bottom, Barbara screamed. She fell back into the dirt, and clawed and screamed as the seven men laughed and cheered around her.

'You're one of us now, Margaret. You've past the test! That one was retarded, touched by the devil himself, so don't worry too much.'

A part of Barbara died that day, and so many times since then, she'd wished that she went over the cliff with the girl. But, an instinct to survive had taken over, and the will to escape the ranch before the same thing happened to her and her sister. Later, she found out that the girl had some sort of disability and she and her mother were picked up by members of the church who found them living in a small trailer at the side of the road. Her mother was very ill, and had tumours in her stomach. She had been extremely worried about who would look after her daughter when she died, and come to the ranch thinking it was the best thing that could ever happen to them, only to be tossed over the quarry edge a few hours later, and her poor daughter sexually assaulted, tortured, and eventually murdered. It was cruelty and evil beyond anything you could imagine.

Back in the present moment, Barbara struggles to tell the priest what she seeks forgiveness for.

'Father I... a long time ago I was in a very difficult, awful situation and somebody forced me to do something I didn't want to. It meant that another person got very hurt and I played a role in that. Although I didn't want to. I was forced.'

Barbara's voice starts to break into a cry and the priest tells her to take a moment.

'This was a very long time ago and I was barely even sixteen years old.'

She starts to weep again, and he leans back in his chair and takes a deep breath.

'You're sorry that this other person was hurt, aren't you? You've been carrying the guilt around for all these years?'

Barbara nods through the tears; she really has been carrying it around, and thought about the girl, and what she'd done to her, every single day. Her heart ached to undo the horrors of the past and to save her.

'We cannot change what has already happened, my child, but God sees and heals a loving soul. Go, pray for your sins, and know that your saviour has forgiven you. Say ten Hail Marys every day for a week.'

And that's it. Barbara stumbles from the confession box, and makes her way slowly to the top of the church to light a candle for the girl. She never even knew her name. Then, the thought enters her mind again that maybe Kate being taken is pay-back for what she did that day in the quarry. Barbara has spent decades running from her past, but its poison has still found a way to the very thing Barbara loves more than anything; her family.

7

Lydia arrives home to be greeted by Molly barking and jumping at the front door. She pops her head into the kitchen to see her dad frying some eggs, but Brian barely acknowledges her in the doorway, and Lydia's heart sinks. He's the most visibly broken out of the three of them right now, she thinks. At least she and her mum can hide behind a layer of make-up, but her dad looks like he's about to keel over and die any second. Brian Stone is a tall man, and always been quite slim, but over the past few months he's just seemed to fade away, no matter how much he eats. Lydia walks over and rests her head gently on his shoulder.

'I love you, Dad. You've taught me that there are good people in the world... and good men, too. I hope you know that.'

Brian is taken aback by his daughter's words. He turns to her, smiles, and kisses her on the forehead.

'Thanks for that, love. You know just what to say to make me feel better. How did things go with your mum?'

Lydia realises that she's been gone for hours, and her dad must think she and mum were together this whole time. Maybe he's worried she'll take her mum's side, and that's why he seems off.

'Oh! Sorry... yeah I met her earlier, and then met a friend for a couple of drinks after that, actually.'

Brian smiles and nods when he hears she's been drinking, and playfully suggests that's the reason she's been so sweet. Lydia laughs with him and takes a seat at the kitchen table.

'Mum's hiding something, isn't she?'

Brian stops what he's doing and asks what Lydia

means.

'Dad, you don't think she's hiding something and not telling us? I know you do, because I've heard you two arguing at night. I've heard you asking her to tell you the truth. That's why she left, isn't it?'

Brian dries his hands with a little yellow towel, pulls out one of the wooden chairs at the table, and sits down across from Lydia. Molly lays at his feet, and he strokes her head.

'You're right Lyds. I've had my suspicions about your mother for a while to be honest, but it wasn't until Kate went missing that I started to feel the need to know the truth about her. I don't know why it took this happening to make me ask questions but... I don't know.'

Lydia asks what his suspicions are; she has no idea what he means, what 'truth' is there to uncover? Brian clears his throat, leans forward, and adjusts his shirt sleeves; procrastinating what he needs to say. He looks at his daughter, and with a gentle voice, explains that he believes her mum is in some sort of witness protection program, and was not born Barbara Kelleher, either. He believes her real name is Margaret. He's found an old bracelet with Margaret engraved on it, and a few months ago he also came across a photograph of Barbara as a teenager with a few other girls and 'Margaret' had been written on the back, along with the names of the others. Every time he had asked her about it, she denied everything, and told him he was being paranoid, but he knew she was keeping something from him, and just couldn't figure out why she wouldn't tell him the truth. Lydia remembers the day the strange man stood across the road from the house and was shouting for Margaret, and her mother had seemed disturbed by the news when Lydia told her about it. She asks her dad if he thinks that man knew her mum from before she changed her name.

'It's very possible, darling. If you ever see him again call me, okay? I don't know who else we could actually ask for answers besides him...'

Her dad's brow is furrowed, and he seems frustrated that he doesn't know more, but Lydia is relieved he's finally talking to her about what's going on. She has a sudden thought.

'What about Jane? Surely, she would know if something was going on? She's Mum's sister after all. Dad we need to talk to her.'

Brian explains that he's already tried with Jane, and she hangs up the phone when he asks about their childhood, who Margaret is, or anything like that. Obviously, Barbara has warned her not to talk.

'Maybe I can try?' Lydia suggests. She takes out her phone and sends her aunt a message.

'Okay! I've asked her to Skype later. She's already mad at me for not talking to her on my birthday, so she's almost expecting this.'

Lydia is actually excited. She picks up one of Molly's chew toys and starts to play with her. The dog jumps and barks; delighted at the attention. Brian has left the room, but returns a few minutes later and puts the bracelet and photograph on the table for Lydia to take a look at. She stops playing with the dog and strokes her with one hand, while picking the photograph up with the other. It's marked 1992. That's six years before she and Kate were born, and three years before Barbara left the United States to come to England.

'Mum's so young here! Oh my god, she's beautiful.'

In the photograph, Barbara is leaning on a wooden fence, her long dark hair is almost to her waist, and she's wearing a white blouse with some sort of detail in the neckline, and tan-coloured shorts. Her skin is very brown, and her smile is wide. She seems genuinely happy, and the other girls alongside her look pretty happy too.

'Any idea who they are?'

She looks to her dad.

'Nope. School friends maybe… or cousins? Your guess is as good as mine, sweetheart. All I know is that 'Barbara' is not listed as being on there, and that's definitely your mother in the picture.'

Brian taps the photograph gently and shakes his head, but Lydia stares at it resolutely.

'Dad, thanks for telling me. I feel so much better now that I know this stuff. Let's keep talking, okay? We will find answers. I just know it.'

8

Kate didn't expect things to change as quickly as they have, but within a couple of days of finding out that she's pregnant, Melvin moves her to a room on the second floor of the farmhouse with a window and double bed. She'll still be chained, but now has fresh air and daylight. The wonderful smells of nature outside the window actually start to cheer her up, and for the first time, Kate knows that she's in the countryside; she can hear cows, sheep, the distant sound of tractors, not to mention the constant birdsong that surrounds the house. But, she doesn't hear any traffic, and thinks this must mean they're in quite an isolated area.

Kate had imagined having children one day, maybe when she was in her thirties, but there's no way she feels ready for anything like that now, at nineteen. But, being in captivity with two psychotic people does things to you, and she actually takes enormous comfort from the little life growing inside her. She starts to sing to her baby; anything she can remember from Disney movies or nursery rhymes, and even starts to make up songs about their future life together. Kate's world has become pretty small, and when that happens, things start to seem more significant. She starts to notice the detail and rhythm of a day, and without a clock, she learns to tell the time based on the light, the sounds from outside, or meal times in the house. She quickly starts to keep track of the days and weeks; the fact that every Sunday Melvin and Christine go to mass in the village, and Kate estimates that because the journey doesn't take long, the village must be close, because they're never gone for more than an hour and a quarter. As far as she knows, it's the only time that both of them leave the house at the same time, and one of them, usually Melvin, rushes to make sure she's still there when they return. Kate imagines that attending mass together is an important thing for the couple to do, and it must give a good impression to the other villagers. Some days, Melvin leaves the house for several hours too, and Kate wonders if he works, but is too afraid to ask, and she decides to wait for him to tell her himself, and also considers the possibility that he has friends somewhere, although that seems unlikely…

Christine is out this evening, and Melvin comes upstairs with Kate's evening meal on a tray. He seems to be in really good spirits and calls out 'Room Service!' as he opens the door. Kate greets him with a smile. She's learned that the nicer she is to him, the nicer he is in return. He sits at the end of the bed, puts the tray down, then unlocks the chain around her wrists. As he's doing it, she sees that there are two plates of food on the tray. He must want to stay and eat with her.

'This looks lovely, Melvin. Thank you. I'm hungry today.'

He seems satisfied with the way things are going, and hands a plate to her. She takes it awkwardly.

'Go ahead.' he says as he picks up his own plate and starts to eat. Kate hasn't eaten with another person like this since before she was kidnapped, and it feels like a privilege. She had spent months sleeping on an old mattress on the floor in the basement, and almost lost her mind with hunger, isolation, and lack of stimulation. Having a bed, daylight, and meals on a tray now, feels almost too good now. It's funny how your perception can change so quickly, and how things that once felt ordinary can feel extraordinary. Kate can't help but feel close to this man. She relies on him for everything; he decides whether she lives or dies. He and Christine have become a strange mix of captors and evil parents to her. Melvin starts to tell her about life on the ranch in Texas; how many people lived there; how crazy a time it was, and how they had to hide from the law to keep the place secure. They also needed to vet anyone who expressed an interest in joining them; they couldn't have afforded to allow any spies in, or anyone that would spread lies about them in the outside world. He speaks about the ranch like it was the best place on earth.

'It was huge and beautiful. We had all these horses and cows... My father was the leader of course, and that meant I was one of the most respected of the men folk.'

Kate looks at Melvin and feels the urge to ask about her mother. He seems to know this.

'You're wondering about her, and her sister, aren't you?'

Kate nods gently and tries to smile at him.

'Only if you want to tell me.'

She's learned that being submissive gets the best results when you're in captivity. Plus, she was good at reading Melvin, and using simple reverse psychology, where she suggests he might want to tell her something more than she wants to know, might just yield the results she longs for; to find out about her mother's past.

'Margaret arrived when she was sixteen years old and I was eighteen. It was perfect. My father had been having the visions for years before that, and we all knew; every single man, woman, and child, when we laid eyes on her that she was the one who would give birth to my child, and save our souls.'

Melvin goes on to speak for almost an hour about

what happened after Margaret arrived at the ranch. He thought that she would be afforded the same luxuries and treatment that he and his immediate family were. He thought he was going to marry her, and they would love one another, but there were men in the group who were suspicious of women, and they were unsure about whether Margaret was really 'the one'. They insisted on putting her through a series of tests before she was allowed to marry Melvin, and if she passed, they would agree that she was the chosen woman, and give their blessing for him to take her as his wife. Kate listens as Melvin describes the men. They sound like clan elders to her; older men who advised Melvin's father, and made all of the laws for the church members. They were misogynists to say the least, believing that the purpose of women was to serve men, and they were cruel to their wives and daughters. They were also involved in lots of other strange rituals that Melvin doesn't want to tell Kate about, but he says they were very unusual and secretive. When Melvin had asked his father about the men, and how cruel they were, his father explained they were the ones who battled with the dark side, and the evil in the world, so that the rest of them could live in peace. Melvin never really understood that reasoning, but he trusted his father, nonetheless.

'What tests did my mother have to pass, Melvin?'

Kate hasn't planned on interrupting him, but she can't help herself. These men sound awful, and she is terrified about what they might have done to her mother.

'They would go off to do their rituals into the mountains for days, or sometimes longer, and they'd take girls with them. Some were only children really, bless them. I remember their mother's faces and the screaming and tears when they left. I guess they needed to weed out the weak ones and... well, not all of the girls made it back.'

Kate is forming a picture in her head. It was obvious that her mother had been taken, raped, and maybe beaten by these men. She was only sixteen years old back then; it must have been devastating. Melvin notices that Kate has started to cry, and looks genuinely concerned.

'You shouldn't be getting upset like this. It's not good for the baby. I'm sorry. You take a few deep breaths and I'll get us both some tea and biscuits, okay?'

9

Lydia's in her room waiting for her aunt to answer the Skype call. When she eventually picks up, Jane looks like she's been crying, and she looks older too and more serious than Lydia remembers. Lydia wonders what's going on in Jane's life; they used to talk all the time, and the two families would visit one another at least once a year. But when the girls reached their teens, things seemed to change, and these days, Lydia didn't have a clue what any of the family in Florida were doing, besides what she sees from the occasional photo one of them posts on social media. Lydia hasn't made any sort of plan about what she's going to ask Jane about exactly, but she needs some sort of confirmation about her mother's previous life, and who 'Margaret' is. After five or ten minutes chatting about what her cousins are up to, she changes the subject:

'You know Mum has moved out, right?'

Her aunt nods, and looks genuinely concerned.

'Your dad said, honey, and I'm so sorry. Did she say why?'

Lydia hesitates. This could be a way in. All she needed was some confirmation that her mum was keeping something from them.

'Well... I think that Dad thinks she's not telling him everything about her past, you know?'

Jane moves about in her seat, takes a drink from a carton of juice, then nods her head in understanding.

'Yeah, that must be hard on you, honey.'

Lydia is irritated already, and feels patronised, but tries to stay calm and casual.

'What do you think about it all, Jane? Do you think Mum is lying to us? Is she protecting us from

---

37

something?'

Jane looks away momentarily, as if planning what to say next.

'I'm not sure what's going on, honey. I don't like to say, okay? It's between your mom and dad.'

Lydia leans forward.

'You don't need to tell me what it is, Jane. But there is something, isn't there… something she's protecting? You know, don't you?'

Jane actually looks shocked. She doesn't say anything for a few seconds, and Lydia thinks that Skype has stalled and frozen the screen, then her aunt looks down, and it seems like she's about to say something. Instead, she looks back at Lydia, her eyes filled with tears.

'I'm not feeling very well, Lydia.'

She closes her laptop and disappears. Lydia gets up and walks to the window. There's no doubt in her mind that Jane knows something. She goes downstairs to tell her dad what's happened, but finds him asleep on the sofa; a heavy astronomy book on his chest. Molly is lying on the floor in front of him, and Lydia calls to her gently.

Once they're on the heath, Lydia lets Molly off the lead, does a few stretches using a bench, and starts to jog slowly. Molly runs along beside her. The insomnia and panic over the past few months has made Lydia weak, and she's determined to improve her health with regular exercise and plenty of good food. When they've run around the duck pond twice, Lydia stops, and stretches again, then starts to walk towards the main road. She puts Molly back on the lead and contemplates walking through the village, but before she can decide if it's a good idea, she spots someone she recognises. It's Ida, the psychic she went to see when Kate first went missing. Ida's already seen Lydia, is waving excitedly, and smiling from across the road. Lydia hasn't thought about her in weeks, but is immediately delighted to see Ida. She starts walking towards her and suddenly feels the urge to tell her about her mum and Jane. Then, Lydia remembers something that gives her chills up and down her neck; Ida had mentioned someone called Margaret when Lydia went to her for a reading all those months ago! It was suddenly all starting to make sense! The pair embrace, Ida tells Lydia that she looks really well, and they chat for a few minutes, then Lydia asks if she might be able to fit her in for a session sometime soon. She tells Ida that there are a few things on her mind, and she could really use some guidance. Ida's face is full of kindness and warmth, her smile makes Lydia feel safe and peaceful. She's still like the grandmother she never had.

'I'm free today. I just need to go to the post-office and pick up some shopping but... I could see you in about an hour or two? Say seven o clock?'

Lydia nods, tells her that seven is perfect, says goodbye, and starts to walk home. There's enough time for a bath and a call to Jared before she heads back out.

10

Kate lies awake. The things that Melvin has told her about her mother and the ranch have made her feel very strange; like she's only just finding out who her mum is, after all these years. There's still so much mystery surrounding her mother's past; for one thing, her name isn't even Barbara. Kate thinks she must have managed to go into some sort of witness protection programme or changed her name by deed poll, and moved to the UK that way. She wonders if her dad knows anything about any of this. What if she married him just so she could stay in England and be safe? Nothing seems impossible or far-fetched anymore. Kate also wonders if her mother was against her modelling career in the beginning because it meant the family would get photographed and have some sort of public profile. The people who were after her, Melvin's family, might find her more easily that way. Then it dawns on Kate; that must be how he found them! How else was it possible? Her heart sinks. She's the one to blame for all of this; if it wasn't for her stupid modelling and wanting to be famous, this never would have happened, and they all could have lived their lives as a happy family.

The moon is bright tonight. Kate cannot see it from the bed, and can't move any closer to the window, but its light finds a way into the room through a crack in the curtains, filling it with a cool hue. She raises up an arm to examine it in the unusual light. Her skin seems a silvery blue, like there's something luminous or ultraviolet in her blood, or some kind of film covering her skin. Kate imagines the moon is transforming her, and giving her strength. It reminds her of some sort of comic book story where an ordinary person gets superhuman powers after a freak accident, like being struck by lightning, bitten by a strange insect, or even swallowing some sort of radioactive substance. She needs something like that to get out of here. Kate decides to tell the baby a story about a girl who was locked in a tower by an evil man and was waiting for a prince to come and save her, until one day she realised that there were no princes left anymore, and instead, she had to save herself. She waited until the moon was at its fullest, then she soaked up all of its wonderful magnetic light.

'Did you know that the moon controls the oceans, baby? It's so powerful that it can tell the seas to flow in to the shore or out. It decides how big the waves are, and even has a role to play when tsunamis happen. The moon might seem small when we look at it from down here, but its power can be harnessed...'

Before she can finish the story, Kate is asleep. She falls into a deep, heavy sleep, and dreams that she's having a picnic on Hampstead Heath with her parents and Lydia. She doesn't hear the arguing from downstairs, or the smashing of plates. The full moon can bring out the worst in people.

11

Christine was convinced that Melvin would give her permission to skip mass this week on account of her bruised face. When he pushed her the day before, she had hit it hard on the corner of the counter top, and it was still bright purple. But Melvin didn't seem to care about how it might look, and told her to tell people she had slipped in the shower. Now, she is starting to feel embarrassed about what the people in the village might think. She is shy and quiet in public, and finds lying very difficult. She practices what she might say in her head, and tells herself that she can pass any blushing off as embarrassment at her own clumsiness.

About an hour before they are due to drive into the village, Christine brings Kate's breakfast to her. On the floral tray sits a small plate of scrambled eggs, two slices of buttered homemade soda bread, a glass of orange juice, and a small egg cup with three different vitamins inside.

'Do you need the bathroom again before we go?'

'I think I'll be okay for a while. Thank you, Christine.'

Kate responds with a smile, and when she looks at Christine, notices the large bruise on her face. Christine feels herself flush red, turns away, and busies herself with fixing the curtains.

'It's going to be a bright day I think, and the wind seems to have died down...'

Kate decides to say something, although her first thought is to ignore the bruise, and play along with the small talk. But she has spent months living under the same roof as Christine, and there is every chance she could be an ally for Kate at some stage. She clears her throat, and waits for Christine to turn around, but she seems to be lost in thought, or is perhaps having a moment to herself. She continues to stand with her back to Kate, staring out the window.

'Did he do that to your face?'

Christine doesn't respond or move. Her eyes stare across the lawn to the woods below. She doesn't like this feeling; this girl speaking to her like she's her equal. Christine turns around suddenly, and looks at Kate straight in the eye.

'I slipped and fell. That's all. Not that it's any of your business.'

Kate gets the message and nods profusely.

'I've done exactly the same thing in the past. I'm so clumsy!'

Christine takes a moment to assess whether Kate really believes her. If she can convince Kate, she can convince the people at mass.

'If you've got any make-up, I can help you cover it for mass?'

Kate takes a bite into the soda bread, and makes an appreciative sound. She doesn't want Christine to feel belittled or self-conscious; that wouldn't be good for anyone, especially Kate. She needs to be her friend now.

'I'll see you later on. Just leave your tray on the ground, okay?'

Kate nods and smiles at her.

'Thanks, Christine.'

Ten minutes later, Christine is back in the room; she's found some make-up that she picked up in the reduced section of the local chemist. She tells Kate that she's never really worn make-up, but is willing to try, if it makes the bruise seem less obvious. Kate has been wearing make-up since she was about twelve, and relishes the challenge of covering Christine's bruise. She squeezes some of the foundation on to the back of her left hand, and mixes it gently with one finger. She reaches out to dab some on Christine's face and begins to blend it in gently. Christine is obviously uncomfortable at being touched. In all of the months that Kate has been here, this is the first time they have done anything that put them on any sort of equal footing. Christine clung to her status of Melvin's wife like it was something to be proud of, and Kate could see that being married to him was her whole world, and all she had, really. It was pathetic, but Kate had to play the game, and tiptoe around the obvious glaring fact that he was a deluded psychopath, and Christine had been beaten and brainwashed into submitting to him for all these years.

'You've got perfect skin, Christine. People would die to have that softness, you know.'

Christine hasn't received a compliment for as long as she can remember, and can't help but smile bashfully. She touches her cheek with one hand, and wonders if she ever really considered something as simple as the softness of her skin.

'Right, I think I've done a good job! Go and take a look, then tell me what you think!?'

Kate hasn't been able to cover the bruise completely, but now you can only really tell it's there when you're close to her. So, people across from her at church won't know. Christine can't believe it.

'That cost me two pounds in the bargain basket! It's a miracle!'

The two women smile at one another, but before

they can say anymore, Melvin's voice booms from downstairs. Christine springs to action and rushes to him without glancing back at Kate.

As she hears their car disappear down the long driveway, Kate smiles and hums to herself; she's not sure what her plan is, exactly, but it feels like things are improving around here. She places both hands on her tummy and looks down.

'For the next hour and a half, it's just you and me, Baby.'

12

Brian returns from a jog at around 10 PM. He hadn't meant to fall asleep on the sofa earlier, and had woken up at eight forty-five to find a note on the kitchen table from Lydia, telling him she'd gone to see Ida, and would have her phone off from seven. The jog has woken Brian up again, and now that he's back home, he's eager to find out how things have gone with Ida. He calls out Lydia's name as he kicks off his trainers in the hall, and gives Molly a pat on the head. There's no answer. Surely Lydia's home by now, he thinks. It's been over three hours since she was supposed to go and see Ida. He picks his phone up from where he left it on the hall table, and calls Lydia's name out once again, before he starts to panic. A few moments later, she appears on the stairs. Her face is paler than usual, and she says nothing, but when she sees her father standing there in his green running shorts and baggy hoody, her eyes fill with tears.

'Darling, you're here. I was wondering.... what's the matter?'

Lydia walks down the remaining steps, and tells him she needs to talk. Brian follows her closely into the living room and they sit on the sofa. Lydia curls her legs beneath her, and hugs a large cushion. Molly comes and licks her face, then lies down in between the two of them. Brian cleans his glasses and awaits his daughter's news. Lydia tells him about her visit to Ida, and how it was the most intense one yet. She had gone there asking about the name 'Margaret' again, and had confided in Ida about her mother moving out and refusing to tell them about her past. She told Ida about the bracelet too, showed her the photograph of her mother when she was younger, and also told her about the strange man who had showed up outside, asking about Margaret. Ida had gone into a sort of trance all of a sudden. It was terrifying. She started seeing things; visions of children, families who were all part of some kind of secret group, and there was a girl among them by the name of Margaret. When she was in the trance, Ida started describing what she could see to Lydia, and it sounded horrific. She said people, mostly children, were killed there, and the group worshipped someone; did sacrifices for them, and Lydia's mother was part of it. After what seemed like half an hour, Ida came out of the trance, drank a lot of water, and used some selenite crystals to clear the room. She saw that Lydia was scared, and consoled her as well as she could, but Ida was sure that it was Lydia's mother she had seen. She was part of this group.

'Dad, I believe her. I think this is real, and Mum won't tell us for some reason.'

Brian's face is grey. He doesn't want to believe what he's hearing, but instinct tells him there's something to it.

'Why is this all coming out? What does this have to do with our lives now, and with Kate?

He hangs his head, and shakes it from side to side in bewilderment.

'Dad... Ida thinks that this group took Kate. She says that every time she taps into Kate's energy, she knows it has a connection to Margaret – to Mum.'

Brian's face is frozen in shock as his daughter's words sink in.

'Dad, Ida thinks Kate is still alive. And I know you do too.'

13

Kate has just finished washing herself with a basin of hot water and a cloth, and Christine has given her a clean pair of leggings and a hoody to put on. Christine hums as she locks the chain around Kate's wrists again, and they both jump when they hear Melvin shout up the stairs. Christine rushes to him, and Kate can hear both of them raise their voices. A few minutes later, Melvin appears at the door and tells Kate there is nothing to worry about.

'You stay calm. We don't want your blood pressure affected or anything.'

Kate asks if everything is alright, and Melvin says that some people in the village are a little bit nosy, but it's nothing he can't handle. Kate is secretly pleased that Melvin is having a hard time; she resents the fact that he gets to saunter in and out of town whenever it suits him and pretend to be this god-fearing, anglophile. But, part of her also wonders if he might be a little stricter with her now that people are being nosy. Perhaps Christine's bruised face was noticed, even through the make-up. The locals must think it's strange that no-one has been in this house, too. Well, no-one has since Kate's been here. Melvin might feel like he needs more control now. Kate uses her excellent instincts, and asks him if she can have a word. She whispers the request softly, and gives Melvin a look that could almost be seen as flirtatious. Thankfully, since she fell pregnant, Melvin hasn't forced her to have sex at all, and Kate feels fairly confident that he now sees her as some sort of blessed baby-vessel, and that makes it safer for her to be close to him.

'Melvin, I've had the most amazing dream. I wasn't

sure if I should tell you...'

Melvin's ears almost visibly prick up at her words.

'Yes? Tell me about it?' he says, as he walks over to Kate.

'Well, in the dream I think I met your father. He came to me and said that he was happy that I was having this baby. He said that God was happy too, and that the prophecy that he had all those years ago was finally happening and he was proud of you, his son.'

Kate can't believe she is going this far. She had toyed with the idea of convincing Melvin she believed his bullshit, and saw it as a way that he would trust and respect her more; perhaps leading to more privileges in the future, or even a chance to escape. She didn't think she would be able to act so believably, but it's as if Melvin is desperate to hear what she has to say, or was waiting for it, somehow. He raises his arms out in front of him, opens his palms so they're facing upwards, closes his eyes, smiles, and begins to pray.

'Praise Jesus. The girl is saved! My son, my son! The one who will save the world, he has touched her sinful blood, and brought her to you, God.'

He opens his eyes and sits next to Kate on the bed, then reaches out and embraces her. Kate forces herself to hug him back although every cell in her body is repulsed by him. She whispers in his ear:

'Thank you for leading me to God.'

That night, Melvin comes back to read the bible to Kate. He stays for over an hour, and when he's finished reading, she thanks him, and bows her head. Before he leaves the room, he wishes her goodnight and Kate smiles back at him sweetly.

'I wish I could go to mass with you and Christine.

Maybe I will one day...'

Melvin doesn't respond, but as he descends the stairs a few moments later, he nods and smiles to himself. He can't believe everything is going so smoothly.

Christine asks what he's been doing when he enters the living room, but he ignores her and puts some wood on the fire. Her words, her voice, irritate him. She starts to say something else, and he interrupts her before she can finish, and tells her to mind her own business. Christine is starting to be more of a hindrance to him these days. She has devoted her life to Melvin, helped him to pass as a regular married man in this country, she has committed a number of terrible acts for him and he still has no respect for her.

14

Brian hasn't told Lydia, or anyone, that he's meeting his wife. He stands outside the pub across from the entrance to Primrose Hill park with two flat whites from their favourite deli. He sips at his nervously. Today, he is meeting the woman he loves more than anyone in the world, the same woman he's been married to for twenty-one years, and he's more nervous than the day he asked her to spend the rest of her life with him. Barbara spots him from across the street and gives a little wave as she walks to him. She nods at the coffees and smiles.

'For me? You're a mind-reader. Thanks! It's cold, huh?'

Brian had psyched himself up to take charge of the conversation and avoid this kind of small talk, but before he knows it, they're discussing the weather and laughing about wearing the wrong thing. They enter the park and Brian suggests walking up the steep path to the view at the top. There are joggers, dog-walkers and tourists around, but plenty of opportunities for Brian to ask what he came to ask without anyone hearing. Still, it takes him a while to pluck up the courage, and it isn't until they are at the top of the hill, and looking out at the view of the grey city in the distance, that he finds a lull in the chit-chat to say what he needs to. He turns to Barbara and tells her that he loves her. She looks back into his eyes, and tells him she loves him too. She seems open today and it spurs Brian on.

'Darling, I need to ask you something, okay?'

Barbara is still looking at him and smiles gently, almost meekly, as she nods her head. She lowers her gaze as one would when they are waiting for some bad news, and it's almost as if she knows what he's going to say next.

'When you lived in the States when you were younger, were you part of any sort of group... like a commune, or a cult?'

Barbara is still looking at her husband, and her eyes fill with tears. She doesn't respond right away, but when she does, her voice is a trembling whisper.

'What is it that you think I am? Or what do you think I know that you so desperately need to know too, huh?'

She's shaking now, but the smile is still in on her face. It's disconcerting to watch, as her composure melts away.

'Lydia has been to see that psychic again, and she believes that Kate is alive. I know you do too, Barbara. We don't know how legitimate this psychic is, but she seems really sure that Kate's disappearance has something to do with your past and is connected to it, somehow. She's having visions Barbara, this lady, and she said she can see you in the past, as part of a group; like an evil sort of cult...'

Barbara is still shaking her head, and takes a few steps back from Brian. She's no longer smiling, and there is a sort of distant coldness in her eyes.

'You blame me for Kate's disappearance! You think that if I was a better mother, and a better person with a perfect upbringing, she would somehow still be here!'

Brian takes a step towards her, but she puts her hands out to tell him to stop. When she speaks again, her voice is shrill, and filled with panic. People are starting to stare at them, and Brian is suddenly aware of a group of teenage boys nearby, laughing at them.

Barbara carries on regardless. She's almost shouting now:

'You never loved me! You used me, and now that your perfect life is failing, and breaking, you're blaming me! And it's killing me, Brian. It's killing me!'

Brian stares in shock at the woman before him. She doesn't even look like his wife anymore. How can she change from calm to manic so quickly? Barbara backs away further, then turns and walks down the steep path towards the park entrance. Brian slumps on to a nearby bench, utterly unsure about what to do next, and watches as she disappears down the path and into the distance.

Barbara hails a taxi from the high street, and is at her rented apartment in Hampstead village in less than ten minutes. Once inside, she walks to the freezer and pulls out a bottle of vodka, pours herself a generous glass, adds some ice and downs it in one, then pours another. She walks slowly and calmly around the flat, swirling the ice around in the glass as she walks. In the weeks that she's been away from Lydia and Brian she's been decorating this new place with them in mind. She runs her hands across the blue cashmere blanket on the back of the sofa and remembers shopping for it, thinking that Lydia would approve. She had even filled the fridge and cupboards with things Lydia liked and had envisaged nights in here watching movies, and finding a way to get close to her again. Barbara tells herself she's a fool for even thinking her family would come back to her. They have already jumped to the conclusion that the sins of her past are somehow responsible for Kate's disappearance. She knew they would turn against her someday. She goes to the bathroom and opens a large black toiletry bag. Inside are four bottles of prescription medication. She picks them up and carries them back into the living area, opens each container, and spills the contents on to the glass top of the coffee table. Suddenly, she's aware that she's sitting close to the window, and anyone could be watching from across the street, so she gets up, pulls the blind down, and switches the Tiffany lamp on in the corner. As Barbara sits back down and continues to pour the pills on to the table, she realises that she feels entirely numb. She has dissociated from her own body; from this room, and can barely remember what it feels like to know sadness, fear or guilt. This is the state she needs to be in to end it all, she decides. When she's sad, missing her family, or feeling shame about the past, she's too connected to life, but this state of numbness allows her to get what she needs done. She takes a handful of pills, swallows them with some of the vodka, then reaches across the sofa, drags her handbag to her, and pulls out her organiser. Inside, are four envelopes; one each for Brian, Lydia, Kate, and Jane. She wrote the letters weeks ago, and inside are pages and pages to each of them trying to explain why she wants to die and how much they mean to her. Barbara has been suicidal for years but it wasn't until Kate went missing that she knew she had to die. It was no longer a longing, but a certainty. In her opinion, the family can't survive or be safe if she is alive. She is poison, and they are all better off without her. She takes another handful of pills and swallows them with the rest of the vodka. She is ready to go. She's already feeling drowsy, lies down, and pulls the blue rug over her. As she feels herself dropping into heavy unconsciousness, Barbara smiles and thinks of her family. She imagines they are all around her, holding her as she leaves this world.

15

Lydia pretends to be asleep when her dad comes home. She doesn't have the energy to talk tonight; she's been watching a DVD box set of Sex and the City in her room for the past hour, and is more than halfway through a bottle of red wine. She's switched on the fairy lights above the bed and drawn the curtains too. She and Kate used to have afternoons like this, where they came home from school, grabbed loads of junk food from the kitchen, and lay on one of their beds watching television, and gossiping, until their parents forced them to come down for dinner or started nagging them about homework. She turns the volume down on the television and hopes that her dad will think she's asleep. A text comes through from him asking if she's eaten, and she quickly replies that she's had some food and is just resting. Lydia has the sudden urge to see Jared. He hasn't texted her back for a couple of hours, so she sends another message asking what he's doing tonight. She can see that he's online and decides to call instead of waiting for him to respond. He doesn't pick up, and Lydia tries again. Still no answer. She sends a message that's just a question mark, then Jared goes offline without responding to that either. Lydia is getting frustrated; it's difficult enough that they hardly ever get to see each other, but it's just plain rude to ignore her for hours like this! She tries to concentrate on the episode she's watching, it's the one where Phoebe introduces everyone to her twin sister and it's one of Kate's favourites, but Lydia has an uneasy feeling in her stomach and can't focus on the show right now. What if Jared has changed his mind about her? Maybe he isn't in love with her after all, or now that he's got to know her better, he doesn't like her… She starts to feel paranoid and insecure, and before she knows it, she's sending message after message to Jared demanding an explanation and telling him how she feels. He ignores every single one. Panic builds in her chest; Lydia longs to get out of the house, but doesn't know what to do with herself, or where to go. This is the kind of thing that would usually make her cry, but she feels frustrated and angry, instead. She picks up her phone and messages Yukio, one of the performers from Haven she met when trying to figure out what happened to her sister. Yukio was always up for going out; and Lydia thinks she might be the perfect distraction from Jared tonight. She responds to her message within minutes, and invites her to a bar in Camden for a gig and drinks. Lydia says she'll see her there and starts to get ready. She feels like dressing up properly tonight and without thinking about it, she swings open the bedroom door and runs down the hall to Kate's room to find something fun to wear.

The room has been kept exactly the same as it was the night Kate disappeared and it still feels like she's still here in so many ways. Kate's energy emanates from every inch of the place; from the furniture, photographs on the walls, the rows of designer shoes and handbags. Lydia already knows what she's looking for; a short black sleeveless dress with peacock feathers adorning the neckline. Kate bought it for a red-carpet event a couple of years ago and Lydia remembers thinking that she would never have the guts to go out in something like that. But these days Lydia cared a lot less about what people thought of her. She finds the dress and admires it for a moment before laying it out on the bed. Then, she opens the closet where Kate keeps her shoes, and chooses a pair of silver ankle boots. They look unworn. Lydia turns them over, and spots a price tag for three hundred and twenty pounds. She always thought that Kate was disrespectful with money, and wasted it on things that she didn't really want. But today, Lydia is happy and excited to have the chance to wear these gorgeous clothes, and she hurries back to her own room to try them on.

16

Ida sits in the conservatory at the back of her house on Pond Street. Angel is sitting on the chair across from her, watching the birds in the trees outside, and sporadically meowing gently at them. It makes Ida smile. She's finding it difficult to think of anything besides the Stone family lately, and the cat's antics are a welcome distraction. She's never felt so involved with the energy of a missing person before. In the thirty years that she's been practising, she's only had visions as flashes; like brief glimpses at something, or the sense of a place. But the visions about Barbara Stone, or Margaret as she believes her real name to be, are intense and all-consuming. There is a fine balance between channelling psychic energy, and letting it take you over, and Ida has to admit that she's struggling with that balance this time. She's exhausted, but knows this family needs help, and she can guide them in the direction of the information they need to figure out where Kate is, and who took her. It's taking some time, though, and the messages she's receiving are often confusing and unclear. Ida takes a large gulp of tea, and then another, closes her eyes, leans back in her chair, and attempts to tap into Kate's energy. She allows her breath to slow down, and concentrates on the stillness within. She asks her higher self to guide her to Kate, and she waits. After a few minutes, Ida starts to sense that Kate is outside somewhere with trees and grass. It's a peaceful place, and she cannot hear anything except birdsong. Again, she asks her higher self to guide her to Kate. She hears something else; a whimpering, then sees a girl with a gag in her mouth. The girl is beaten and bloody. Ida's face crumples with sadness and empathy for this poor soul. Again, she asks her higher power to lead her to Kate, and the girl's face becomes visible. It looks like Kate, but it's not her. Ida struggles to see more detail, but the vision is blurry. She sees the girl wince as she's struck with something over the head and collapses. Ida's eyes open in shock, and she is momentarily back in the room. She forces herself to close them again and sees the girl lying on the ground, her head covered in the blood seeping from her skull. She can't take any more, and opens her eyes, jumps from her chair, and walks to the downstairs toilet. She splashes water on her hot face and tries to breathe evenly, but adrenaline is pumping through her veins. The girl she saw was murdered. It wasn't Kate, and it wasn't Margaret, but she was somehow connected to all of this.

17

Lydia is drunk. It's not even ten thirty, but she's already asking Yukio where they can go dancing after the bar they're at stops serving. The band they had come to see, has finished their set, and there's a lull before the DJ starts.

'Hold your horses, wild girl! There's plenty of fun people here, and nothing is stopping you from dancing, either.'

Yukio has been at a fashion show at Cyberdog in Camden Stables, and is wearing a tiny cropped t-shirt with LED lips on it. Lydia points and laughs at the t-shirt, then twirls with her eyes closed, and raises her glass in the air. She feels high, like she's taken something, and sways to a rhythm only she seems to be aware of. She knows a few of the others in the group from the night she went to Haven in May: Dee, Ian, and Naomi, and she feels at home in the group. After her fifth drink, Lydia starts dancing wildly next to the bar. She shouts across at the DJ who has only just started, to turn the volume up, and the group laugh at her behaviour. The first night they all went out together Lydia was sweet and shy for the most part. This all seems very out of character for her. She spots a cute guy across the bar, with curly hair and a leather jacket, and without thinking twice, goes over to him, puts her arm around his neck and shouts in his ear that she wants to kiss him. The young man, seeing how drunk she is, politely thanks her for the compliment, then points out his girlfriend who's glaring at Lydia in a not-so-friendly way. She mumbles something at them and finds herself laughing hysterically as she stumbles to the toilets. She almost falls into a cubicle, and once she's inside, she sits on the toilet seat, drops her purse on the floor and rests her head in her hands. Dizziness and nausea are soon to follow… After about ten minutes Yukio comes to find her and knocks on the door. Lydia emerges, staggers to the basin to splash some water on her face, and apologises.

'I'm so drunk, Yukio! I'm going to get a taxi home, okay?'

'Sure honey, I can call one for you and make sure you get in safe, okay?'

Then Lydia has a thought.

'Actually... I've got a boyfriend now... he can come get me!'

She finds her phone in her bag and calls Jared. As it's ringing, she hands the phone to Yukio and rushes back into a cubicle to throw up. Lydia doesn't even hear what Yukio is saying, but twenty minutes later, Jared helps Lydia into the passenger seat of his car and drives her to his flat. He is not happy.

Just a few miles away, Barbara is on her way to A&E. She had woken up when she started vomiting, managed to grab her phone to call 999, and told them she had attempted suicide and what her address was. Brian gets the call from the hospital at around 11.30, and at first, thinks it's got something to do with Kate, and then he remembers Lydia is out. He's still half asleep and it takes longer than usual to understand what the nurse is saying down the phone. All he hears is that his wife is unconscious and has taken an overdose.

He's at the Royal Free Hospital in twenty minutes and sitting by her bed.

'Mr Stone, has your wife done anything like this before?'

'No, never.'

'Any idea if she's on any medication or has been diagnosed with anything? How long has she been suicidal?'

Brian is flustered; he doesn't want to give any incorrect information to the nurse, but as far as he knows, Barbara doesn't even take pain relief for a headache.

'We are separated for the moment. Temporarily. And... to be honest with you I don't know if she's on any medication. We've been through some family trauma recently. Our... our daughter Kate is missing, and has been since May, and it's taken its toll.'

As Brian is talking, the reality of the situation hits him. He could have lost Barbara tonight. The nurse notices how upset he is and tells him that a member of the mental health team is available to chat to him, as well as the hospital chaplain.

'We are waiting for someone from our psychiatric department to come and see your wife, Mr Stone, but it will probably be tomorrow morning before that happens. They need to assess her when she wakes up. We'll be in touch as soon as we know anything, but she's safe and stable right now, and we'll make sure she is comfortable in the night.'

Brian kisses Barbara on the forehead, and whispers that he loves her and will be back first thing in the morning. By the time he gets home it's after 1AM. There's no sign of Lydia, so he sends a text to see if she's okay. An hour later there is no response, and he decides to give her a call. Her phone vibrates in her handbag, unnoticed.

18

The next morning, Lydia wakes up before Jared, and furiously tries to piece the night together. He's got his back to her, and even though he's asleep, she can tell by his body language that he's not happy with her. Then she remembers her dad, and reaches for her bag and phone. There are sixteen missed calls from him, and numerous text messages asking where she is and if she's okay. She texts back immediately saying she fell asleep at a friend's place and will be home soon. As she collects her things from the floor, Jared sits up in the bed.

'This can't happen again, Lydia.'

'I know. I'm so sorry. I can't believe I called you!'

'It can't happen again, and it won't, because you and I are over, okay? It's just not working for me anymore, and I never should have let things go this far.'

Lydia cannot believe what she's hearing.

'What about everything you said? What about us, and the future? You told me you loved me! Does that mean nothing now because I made one stupid mistake?'

Her voice rises to a frantic pitch, and she climbs on to the bed, holding her face with her hands as she bursts into tears. As much as she felt hurt that Jared had been distant lately, she had no idea he was capable of dumping her like this.

'Jared, I'm sorry. Let me fix this? We're in a bad place, but please don't turn away from me like this.'

She reaches out to take his hand, but he pulls away before she can touch him.

'I'm really sorry Lydia. You're amazing. You really

are, but some things are not meant to be, and the timing here, and the age gap. It just doesn't work. Not to mention the fact that I could get into serious trouble at work if they knew. There's just no way.'

Lydia goes from initial shock and sadness to a sort of heavy numbness. For a moment, she thinks she's going to faint, but she manages to get off the bed, collect her things, and get dressed. Before she leaves the room, she turns to Jared one last time, and in a weak matter-of-fact voice, tells him that he's broken her heart. Outside, on the street, Lydia takes a deep breath, and contemplates the fastest route to the underground station. Her phone rings and she's actually relieved to see it's her dad. His voice is bound to make her feel better, and bring some normality to the strange, empty feeling she has in her gut.

'Dad!'

'I have some news. Your mother is in the hospital, Lydia. She... she took an overdose last night...'

His voice continues to explain what happened, but Lydia can't hear him. It sounds like he's just saying random words and isn't speaking loudly enough.

'Lydia? Darling, are you still there?'

She feels the familiar wave of cold panic come over her. Her heart is beating so loudly and quickly that she feels it's going to burst from her chest. She manages to ask which hospital her mum's in, and hangs up the phone. As if by a miracle, a taxi comes towards her, and she flags it down.

19

Kate's baby bump is showing, and her clothes are becoming too tight. For a few days, she's been trying to pluck up the courage to ask Christine to find her something else to wear, and eventually, this morning, she manages to, after her shower. Christine actually seems glad to help, and when Kate is back in the bedroom a few minutes later, she offers to leave her hands untied for a while so she can try on the jumpers and long-sleeved thermal top she has left on the bed. Christine must have got them from her room while Kate was finishing in the shower. Melvin still insists that Kate's wrists are tied together in front all of the time, apart from while she uses the bathroom or changes her clothes in the bedroom, and Christine watches her every move. But, both Christine and Melvin are starting to trust her more; she can just feel it. Over the months, they've started to see her as one of them, and ever since she claimed to have that prophetic dream and started praying, they definitely look at her in a new light. Up to now, Kate has only had a few items of clothing to wear, so it's a bit of a novelty to have some new things. The thermal top looks unworn to her, and sits comfortably over her swelling stomach. Christine seems genuinely pleased that she can help, and tells Kate that Melvin approves of their friendship and wants Christine to help as much as possible right up to the birth.

'We could begin to think of one another as sisters, you know?'

Kate asks Christine if she knows anything about pregnancy and birth, or has ever been around for the birth of a child but Christine shakes her head apologetically. In the next breath, she tells Kate that there's nothing to worry about and she's going to get some books from a nearby town this weekend.

'We can study them together and make sure we know everything that will happen.'

Kate knew that this was going to be the plan; she knew that there was no way Melvin would allow her to go to a doctor, or have her baby in hospital. The risk was too great that she would try to escape or tell someone what was going on. But as time went by and she felt her body change and her baby grow inside her; she couldn't help but imagine the worst. What if there was a complication? So many things could go wrong. Kate didn't know a lot about giving birth, but she knew that sometimes women had to have C-sections and have their babies cut out of them if a vaginal birth was not possible, or would put the baby or mother's life at risk. Kate already knew that her life was only worth something to Melvin and Christine because she was going to give birth to a baby they thought was the next Messiah. If something happened to her in childbirth, they probably wouldn't even care. In fact, they might be planning on killing her as soon as they had their baby anyway. That thought had been lingering at the back of Kate's mind the whole time; these people had been around dark things in the past, and they lived entirely outside of the law. They didn't care about her. She was just part of their story; this religious fantasy, and delusion that they had fed their whole lives, and as soon as she had given birth they would very likely try to dispose of her.

Christine sits on the bed with Kate after she has retied her hands and feet.

'Can I tell you something?'

Her voice is meeker than usual. Kate nods, and smiles gently.

'Of course, Christine. Anything. I'm your friend. What is it?'

Christine hesitates, and looks down at her hands in her lap. Her eyelids flicker a couple of times, and Kate can see that she's crying.

'What is it. Please? You know you can trust me. I'm here for you, okay?'

Christine looks at her for a moment, as if she's checking she's telling the truth. Kate's eyes are large and warm, her skin is glowing. Even as a captive in this strange place, without a friend, and with little hope of a future, Kate's energy, beauty, and life-force is undeniable. Christine sees a good face and one that she can trust. But Kate is not prepared for what she has to say next...

'You're not the first girl to come here. So, it took me a long time to trust that you were the one, and this was real.'

Kate can't believe what she's hearing.

'Melvin can't know that I've told you, but about a year before he got you, he took another girl from a town a few miles away. She was like you; beautiful, young... Melvin saw her late at night on the road and he felt God telling him to stop the car and, h-he took her, and brought her here.'

Kate knows by Christine's voice that they murdered this girl. All of the saliva disappears from her mouth, and her stomach feels heavy. She manages to ask about what happened, and at least appear to stay calm, but her mind keeps returning to the thought that whatever happened to this other girl could easily happen to her, too.

'She was different to you in temperament, and she fought back too much. After just a few days, Melvin knew he'd made a mistake taking her... he hurt her real bad and...'

Christine is shaking. She's obviously scarred by what happened with the girl.

'Christine, please tell me. It's okay. It's not your fault.'

'She was bleeding so badly from her mouth and ears, and she just wouldn't come round, so we had to... put her out of her misery. Melvin realised he had made a mistake and never should have taken her. That's why making it work with you is so important to us.'

Kate feels physically sick. She uses every ounce of her strength to keep up the pretence that she's not judging Christine, but now she knows for a fact that Melvin is capable of extreme violence, and he has already murdered someone with his wife's help.

'Are there any more girls, Christine?'

'Oh, not here. No. Maybe... in some other places, but not here.'

Kate is confused. What does she mean by other places?

'Are there other girls somewhere else?'

Christine stands up, brushes her skirt and apron with her hands, and takes a deep breath. Melvin starts to make some noise downstairs and calls out for her.

'I've said too much. The most important thing to know is that you are the one, Kate. Alright? Everything is going to be good from now on. I'll tell you when I am going to get those books and we can read them together.'

With that, she's gone, and Kate sits in the quiet room, letting all that she has just heard sink in. Now, she has a secret with Christine, which is a good thing. But her captors are murderers! And what did Christine mean when she spoke about other girls? This didn't make any sense. Were there more people like Melvin and Christine all over the place, just taking girls? Perhaps the people from the ranch had simply moved; scattered across the world instead of all living together in a commune? Did others know that she was here? More than ever, Kate knows that she's got to start thinking about an escape. She has built up trust with Melvin and Christine, and done a good job at convincing them she wants to be here and become part of their prophecy and future. Now, she needs to make a plan.

Downstairs, Melvin is in a good mood. A few men from the village had invited him for a drink and he had spent an hour talking about fishing with them. It had erased any doubt in his mind that anyone in Southam knew they were up to anything. He had also got some money deposited to his bank account from the US, and although he didn't want to tell Christine how much, exactly, she could see by his face that it was more than he'd expected.

'I might change the car, and I need you to make a list of things we need for the baby. '

He glances at the ceiling, towards Kate's room.

'See if she needs anything specific or whatever. I want to get it in one trip, so don't be afraid to put everything we need on there. The vitamins and nappies and baby clothes. I'll go alone, and I'll pay in cash.'

Christine nods in approval, and tells Melvin that she'll start on the list straight away.

20

Lydia sits with her mother at the hospital. They've given Barbara some strong medication, and she's barely conscious, never mind making any sense. Lydia asks the nurse when they're going to start seeing any improvement; she can't have a conversation with her when she's like this; and on the occasions that she does seem awake or more alert, Barbara just cries. Lydia asks her why she took the overdose and she just tells her in a matter-of-fact way that she couldn't go on anymore; that her heart was too broken, and she had been struggling for too long.

'It's not your fault, darling. You would be happier without me. All of this is my fault. I was never a good enough mother, and your father has just been putting up with me.'

Lydia is not sure she can even stand to listen to her mother saying these things. She tells herself that what she's hearing isn't true. It just can't be.

'Mum, do you believe that Kate's alive?'

Silence.

'Well I do. I know it in my heart. And when she comes home, because she will be coming home, you better be there.'

Lydia goes out into the hallway, and sees her dad leaning against a wall. She didn't know he was waiting for her, although he had walked with her to the hospital. He looks lost, not like himself, even his body language is different to normal. Lydia leans on the wall next to him, and tells him that her mum is still zombie-like and miserable.

'She needs to stay in there. I'm scared she'll do it again, Dad'

Brian turns to look at his daughter. His face shows how heartbroken he is, and how sorry he feels for her, but, he doesn't expect to see her looking back at him the way she is. She always surprised him when she got like this; sometimes she managed to find a strength he didn't know she had.

'Dad, I'm going to Florida to see Jane. I'm going to book my ticket and hopefully fly tonight or in the morning.'

'What? Why?'

'I can't explain it fully, but I just feel that she might give me some answers if I see her face-to-face, you know? She knows something. I could tell when I skyped with her the other day.'

Lydia was already planning on the trip to see Jane. The only thing that would have changed her mind is if her mother started talking, but that wasn't going to happen, and Lydia feels like it's in her power to get some answers. The thought crosses her mind that maybe it was a good thing Jared had dumped her. She needed to concentrate on her sister.

21

Ida is still being haunted with visions of Kate and the other murdered girl. She is having problems sleeping and started to walk around Hampstead village in an attempt to tire herself out in the evenings. This afternoon, she sits in front of the television and tries to concentrate on a sitcom; something she rarely enjoys. She's trying everything and anything she can to snap herself out of this black mood, but every half hour or so, she has a flash vision of something awful. The visions are aural too, or sometimes all of her senses are engaged, and she can even smell the place. She sees the basement she first saw when Lydia came to her about her missing sister. That was almost six months ago now, and she was still seeing it; this place where Kate Stone was. Surely, this could only be happening if Kate was alive? The other girl that she saw in the visions was probably one that had gone before her. They looked similar, with the same big dark eyes, slender physique, and long, dark hair.

Ida has seen a lot in the seventy-seven years she has been on this earth. She has had run-ins with some dark entities, been moved and changed by some of them, but she's never been haunted by something the way she's haunted by this. She would bet her life on Kate Stone being alive and connected to another murdered girl. But who can she tell about it? The police don't take psychics seriously, and even the few that do have to do so in private. Plus, she has nothing concrete to go on. She picks up her phone and scrolls to find Lydia's number; it's not like her to do this, but she needs to let Lydia her what's happening, and maybe if they did another session, a clear message, or some kind of sign might come through. She gets through to Lydia's voicemail and leaves a message asking her to give her a call when she has a moment. She doesn't want to worry the poor girl; she's probably going through enough as it is, so Ida adds that it's not an emergency, she just wants to check in and say hello.

22

The next morning Lydia calls Ida from the taxi. She's on her way to Heathrow.

'Sorry I didn't get back to you last night. I was packing for Florida actually. My flight is at noon. I'll be gone for a few days.'

She didn't plan on telling Ida anything about the trip. In fact, she hadn't even thought about her since the last visit to her house, but Ida had obviously been thinking about her. Lydia feels a pang of guilt, and can hear that the woman is genuinely concerned. She asks if she can come and see her when she gets back, then they say their goodbyes and hang up. Almost immediately, Lydia sends her a text to say thanks again, and let her know that she'll fill her in if she uncovers anything in the States about her mother's past, or if anyone knows anything about Kate. Then, without giving it a second thought she texts Jared. It's been three days since he told her it was over, and they'd had no contact since. She types: 'Just wanted to let you know I'm off to FL to see my aunt for a few days. Hope you're okay x'. As soon as she presses send she feels better, and breathes a sigh of relief. When the phone rings and she see Jared's name a few seconds later, she feels her heart beat quickly in her chest. She was barely expecting a reply to the text, never mind a phone call.

'Hello'

'Lyds, are you okay? You're going to the States? How come? Is everything alright?'

He's rambling slightly, and sounds flustered.

'Hey. Yup. I'm okay.'

Lydia finds herself giggling at him the way she

usually does.

'Wow, it's nice to hear your voice, Jar.'

'It's nice to hear you too, Lyds.'

She can hear it in his voice that he's smiling. Her heart fills with emotion, and she's not sure what to say.

'How come you called me? I don't know why I texted...'

'No! No! I was so happy to hear from you. It's been a few days, but, gosh it feels like longer.'

'Well, why didn't you text me, then?'

Lydia can feel herself gently teasing him like she is used to doing, and before they know it, they've been chatting for forty minutes and she's almost at the airport. She tells him she's got to go.

'Wait, Lyds? Call me when you get there? I want to talk to you about us.'

Lydia has to hold her mouth to stop from weeping. These are the words she's been longing to hear.

'Yeah?'

'Yeah. Lyds, I love you. Safe flight okay?

Lydia smiles the whole way through check-in and security.

23

Jane didn't answer her phone when Lydia called the night before to tell her she'd booked her flight. Instead, she listened to the voice message, cursed under her breath, and called her sister. But Barbara's phone was off. Jane would have to make a plan on her own, and make sure that Lydia didn't cause any trouble for the family while she was here.

When the doorbell goes at lunch time, she takes a deep breath. She wants to do her best to be a good aunt to Lydia, but what she's looking for isn't in Florida. She isn't going to get any answers here. Lydia had slept on the flight, and all things considered, actually feels quite fresh. It's been years since she's been to see them in Orlando, and this is the first time she's flown here, or anywhere on her own, and she feels free, confident, and totally grown up. The smiling American way is really helping her mood, too. Not to mention the sunshine. The door opens, and Lydia finds herself squealing when she sees her aunt's face. She loves her. No matter what she's hiding, she loves her. Yet, it isn't until she sees Jane that she realises just how much she loves her. She looks like a slightly taller, plumper version of her mother.

'Aunt Jane! You look amazing! I can't believe I'm here!'

Jane finds herself literally jumping for joy when she sees her niece.

'Oh my goodness, you are so beautiful! The photographs don't do you justice.'

Jane reaches out and tenderly touches her niece's cheek, and runs her fingers through the ends of her hair. It's been two years since she's seen her.

'My oh my, this hair is unbelievable! Which products do you use? Who am I kidding? It's all in the genes huh? Your mom's hair. Oh my gosh...'

Lydia and Jane are actually very similar in personality. Neither of them had noticed it before, but there is also something about their energy, their understated, slower way of acting that is alike. They are thinkers, whereas Lydia's mother is more reactive and animated, as is Kate. Lydia has come here seeking answers about her mum, but she has a feeling that she is also going to benefit from just being around her aunt. But, it's weird being around someone you've known your whole life and never spent any one-on-one time with, Lydia thinks. There is a sense of ease and understanding between them, but Lydia knows that if her aunt is like her, she could be just as guarded, if not more so. Jane tells her that her daughter, Lydia's cousin, Jenny will be coming over soon, and Lydia realises that she still has to tell her aunt about what happened with her mum, and that she's in the hospital. She asks her to sit with her in the living room, and explains what happened and that they are all really worried. Jane is visibly upset at the news, and tells Lydia that she had no idea this was going on. If she had known she would have been there on the next flight to London.

'Honey, I just thought she was having problems with your dad. She's never told me about mental health issues, or anything like that.'

Lydia goes straight for it, and tells her aunt that she knows that there's something in her mother's past that she's keeping from everyone, and she needs Jane to be honest with her. But, before her aunt can respond, the front door opens, and a squealing cousin Jenny bounces into the room. Jenny is all hoop earrings and dimples. She reminds Lydia of a cabbage patch doll who's had too much caffeine. She's adorable, excitable, and wears her heart on her sleeve, but she's also the kind of person that Lydia tires of very quickly.

24

Kate lies awake. She knows that she's waited long
enough, and needs to make a plan to escape this place.
Melvin keeps a couple of dogs outside the house, and
she's pretty sure they aren't tied up. One is called Ned
and the other is called Rascal. Kate's heard him
shouting their names. Their meal times and morning
walk are things she's used to hearing, too, and they've
become markers in the day. Melvin shouts at them like
they're wild horses he's trying to tame, yelling 'Heyah!
Heyah!' every time they go through the gate. Kate
thinks that maybe she would be better off trying to
escape during their morning walk; that way she won't
have to worry about them barking, or attacking her. At
that time, Christine would be the only other person in
the house, too, and less likely to be able to stop Kate if
she caught her, and hopefully less violent than Melvin
would be in that scenario. But, the first thing Kate
needs to be able to do is detach herself from the long
metal chain that connects her hands to the heavy bed
frame. Without the ability to free herself from that,
there's no way she's going to be able to go anywhere.
She's never been downstairs either, or seen through the
windows properly, and she has no idea how difficult it
will be to get from the house to a public road. She
knows there is a gate with a lock, and an outside space
like a garage, but she doesn't know if there is another
perimeter around the house, like trees or a wall. For all
she knows, Melvin could have security cameras or
motion sensors out there, too. Plus, she has no idea
what the windows and doors are like downstairs and
how easy it would be to get through them, even if she
did manage to free herself from the chains. She needs to

convince Melvin and Christine that they can trust her enough to have the chains off for at least a portion of the day. That way, she might have some chance of at least looking around the house and seeing if an escape route is possible. And maybe, just maybe, if she can build up their trust, they might allow her stop wearing them altogether.

About twenty miles away from where Kate is lying, a woman in her forties by the name of Annie Latter is lying awake too. She's used to pretending to sleep next to her husband, and doesn't want to take the tablets the doctor has prescribed; she'd rather have her wits about her as much as possible. Since her daughter, Melanie went missing last year, Annie has been working day and night to find her. Before all of this happened, she had no idea just how many people went missing in the UK every year; the police and media kept it quiet for the most part, but people were going missing all the time, seemingly disappearing into thin air. And good people like Annie Latter and her family were not given answers about where they might be. She had read the statistics about sex trafficking and spoken to some experts in the field, and it seemed that this was the most likely thing that had happened to Melanie. She was fifteen when she went, and it was coming up to her seventeenth birthday soon. Annie still hoped she was alive of course, and still spoke to her every single day. Every time the phone rang, every time someone called out Annie's name, she imagined it was news of Melanie. Of course, when Kate Stone went missing it was all over the news. Kate was a celebrity, with a massive circle of friends, and a public profile. It made Annie angry that her case was getting all this attention, and she felt bitter that Melanie somehow wasn't interesting enough for the media to talk about. She had seen photographs of Kate and realised how similar she looked to Melanie; the same long, dark hair, full lips, and large dark eyes. Kate was a little bit taller than Melanie, and thinner than her too, but they were alarmingly alike. Annie met Barbara and Brian Stone at a support meeting in London a few months ago. They reminded her of herself and her husband Rupert in the months after Melanie went missing. They were ghost-like, broken-hearted, and vacant. She had felt connected to them, and wished them luck in finding Kate. Part of her imagined Melanie, Kate, and all of the other missing girls were in the same place. She had to imagine they were alive; the alternative was too devastating. Plus, Annie had two other teenagers at home who needed her to be strong.

By some cruel coincidence, Kate is thinking about Melanie at that same moment. Of course, she doesn't know her name. All she knows is what Christine decided to tell her; that a girl was brought here before Kate was, and they beat her to death. Kate has felt sick and haunted by this fact ever since Christine told her, and she had been too scared to bring the subject up again, although part of her longed to know if she had died in the basement where Kate had been kept for all those months. How long she had been in there for? And, what they had done with her body? Kate had started pretending to pray, in order to convince Melvin and Christine that she was a deserving person in their divine plan. But she had actually started to use the time to speak to her parents, Lydia, and the world in general. She knew that she was technically talking to herself, but it brought such relief. She asked the universe for strength. She asked her family and friends to believe in her, and to never stop loving her. This new knowledge about Melanie had scared Kate, and was the catalyst to push her into forming an escape plan herself. The likelihood of ending up like Melanie was high; the only thing keeping Kate alive was the life growing inside of her. Once she had this baby, her baby, inside of her, Melvin wouldn't be able to harm her. A thought occurs to Kate. She is giving this baby life, and it is giving her life. 'Symbiosis' she whispers in the dark, as she remembers learning what that word meant at school. It was when two systems or beings benefited mutually from their interaction.

'Symbiotic mother and baby.'

She smiles at the memory of the dusty old science lab and her eccentric science teacher, Mr Carr. She had really enjoyed learning about the anatomy of the human body; the kidneys, heart, and eyes. She loved drawing and labelling them. It was therapeutic. What she wouldn't give to be able to draw now. Kate wonders if she will ever get the chance to teach her baby any of this stuff. She can feel her bond growing for this child every day, and had no idea that you could form something so strong, so sure, so fierce; something so glorious, with someone you had never even met before. Kate smiles to herself, and wonders how much hormones have to play in all of this. This baby was also genetically related to a psychotic rapist and murderer, yet it didn't feel like it was one bit Melvin's. It was Kate's baby, and she had to fight for it.

25

Lydia and her cousin Jenny are reminiscing about fun times they had together as kids. Jenny is a very emotional person, and has already cried three or four times about Kate. She tells Lydia that she had to take a week off work when they first found out that she was missing, and she'd been praying for her a lot at their local church. Lydia isn't sure why, but she finds Jenny really irritating. She had never realised this before, but it seems like her aunt Jane feels the same, even though Jenny is her own daughter. Jane continually tells Jenny to change the subject if she's asking too many questions, and eventually suggests that she come back in the morning after Lydia has had some rest, and recovered from her flight. Lydia is relieved; all she wants to do is speak to Jane, alone, and as soon as Jenny leaves, she suggests they order some pizza and open a bottle of wine. Lydia hadn't even planned on saying that; it was as if the words just came out of her mouth, but her aunt is delighted with the suggestion. Her eyes actually light up.

'I've been on a goddamn no-carb diet for the past two weeks, so, pizza? Hell yes! Why don't I order it while you get settled in your room? It's the front one with the long mirror on the door. It's got an ensuite, so freshen up or whatever, and yell if you need anything, okay?'

Lydia immediately feels warm around her aunt. She had never really appreciated her before, but she was kind of fun. It was like all the best bits of hanging out with her own mother, but without the emotional baggage.

Upstairs, Lydia throws her small suitcase on the

bed, and takes out her phone. She calls her dad and tells him that everything is great, Aunt Jane is doing okay, and says hi. She tells him that she's going to do her best to get some answers, and will let him know if she finds out anything. Brian tells Lydia that he's at the hospital with her mum, but hasn't said anything about her being in Florida because he doesn't want her worrying. Lydia agrees, and asks him to say that she's not feeling well for a couple of days and that's why she can't come to visit. Brian is hesitant about lying like that, but eventually agrees. Before they hang up, he tells Lydia he's proud of her, and loves her very much.

A few minutes later, Lydia presses the power button on the shower, and takes her t shirt and jeans off, then picks her phone up again and sends a text to Jared. Determined to play it cool this time, she keeps it short; just telling him she arrived safe and sound, is having a nice time with her family, and is free tomorrow if he wants to talk. In the shower, Lydia makes a plan about what she's going to say to Jane. She feels confident that her aunt trusts her now, and can see that she's not a little girl anymore. Then, a strange feeling washes over her; she can feel her sister's presence. Lydia hasn't felt like this in some time, maybe a month, and it takes her by surprise. She suddenly remembers the night she went to Haven a few weeks after Kate went missing, and thought she saw something in a mirror, and then later that night she saw a figure that looked like Kate in her bedroom by the window. The last thing she wants is to feel scared right now; she's happy to have Kate with her to give her strength. But something feels wrong. Why is it that being in the water makes her feel like this? There's something about this element that makes her feel more in tune with the paranormal, and it's strange because being in Florida means that she's even further away from Kate than ever. Assuming she's still alive, and in the UK. Lydia can feel herself shaking, even though the water in the shower is piping hot.

'Get it together, Lydia. Pull yourself together.'

Then, she does something she hasn't done in a long time. She talks to her sister. Lydia pretends that Kate is right there with her, and she tells her how much she loves her, misses her, and how sorry she is that they haven't found her yet. Tears mix with the hot water running down Lydia's face. The doorbell rings downstairs, and for a second, Lydia thinks Jenny has returned, but then remembers the pizza. It's probably the delivery guy. She turns the shower off, and grabs a towel just as she hears her aunt calling up the stairs to her.

'Gimme five! Coming!' she shouts back.

A few minutes later, Lydia runs down the stairs in fresh clothes. Her hair is still wet, but tied back in a neat bun. She's ravenous, and grabs a giant slice of pizza and a paper plate from the table in the living room. Her aunt is visible through the double doors in the kitchen, and asks Lydia what she wants to drink.

'I'm having a diet soda. Want one?'

Lydia nods. God, she loves America. She loves the sheer amount of food that seems to be available at all times. The triple cheese giganticness of the whole thing. The first time she and Kate went to Disneyland as children, she actually cried with happiness; first when she saw Mickey Mouse and Pluto singing 'Zippidydooda' and skipping towards her, and secondly when she was handed the biggest cookie she had ever seen in her life. She and Kate asked their parents if they could live in Disneyland, and Kate told them all that she was going to get a job singing with the princesses when she was older. Kate loved having family in America and hoped to one day live there for a while.

Jane comes back into the room, and smiles as she places the giant red plastic cups of diet coke on the glass table.

'Do you remember when you used to be obsessed with Dr Pepper and M&Ms? It seems crazy now because you can probably get that candy in England, right? I mean it's not a big deal any more, is it? But you and Kate used to fill your suitcases with the stuff when you went back home, like it was treasure.'

Lydia can't help but laugh. She tells her aunt that she has so many happy memories of being here with Kate when she was little. When the pizza is almost gone and Jane tells Lydia she is officially on a carb high, Lydia decides it's time to change the subject to her mum. She tells Jane about Ida the psychic, and that she believes that her mother's real name is Margaret. She tells her about the man that turned up outside the house a few months ago asking for someone called Margaret, and then the fact that her dad found a bracelet with the same name in her mum's jewellery box. And there was the photograph too.

'Jane, why won't you tell me? What do you have to lose? My sister was kidnapped in the middle of the night from a club, and this might help her....'

Lydia sees her aunt's vacant look. It's the same one that her mother had when she tried to talk to her in the pub that day. Just when Lydia thinks she is never going to say anything, and maybe the whole trip was a mistake, Jane turns her head and looks at her. Her eyes are warm, open, watery with love and sadness. Is she finally going to tell her something?

'Sweetheart. I totally see where you are coming from. All this stuff about someone called Margaret and your mom not wanting you to know about her past... that does seem weird. I would be freaked out too, you know? But what does it have to do with Kate? I don't see how there's a connection.'

Lydia tells her again about the psychic, and her aunt just shakes her head. She seems to think that if a psychic is the only person linking Kate's disappearance to her mother's secrecy about her past, it isn't a good enough reason for all this fuss.

'Honey, I'm going to bed. If you really want to find out about our childhood here in America, take a look in the bureau under the stairs. There's a whole load of photographs of us when we were kids. You'll see two happy girls and two normal-looking parents: your grandparents. We were happy, christian folk who just happened to move around a lot. Your granddaddy had travelling feet, and he never settled anywhere.'

Jane hums to herself and starts to tidy up. Lydia can see that she's not going to get any answers from her this evening. She wishes her goodnight, and waits for about twenty minutes before taking a look at the bureau in the hall.

There are about seven photo albums in total, and Lydia flicks through them for a few minutes before having an idea; she needs to find proof that her mother's real name is Margaret; that's enough to tie her to the bracelet and the weird man looking for her at the house a few months back. If her aunt catches her she might be mad, but Lydia starts to go through every photograph on every album page, peeling it out, and looking at the back. The first ten or fifteen photographs are blank, then one or two have dates and places on them. Lydia takes photographs of these with her phone. She's not sure why, but wants them just in case she needs to build a picture of where they moved to over the years. She can see her mother's features change almost overnight, and she suddenly looks mature. Lydia continues to remove each photograph, check the back for any sign of a name, and then replace it. Eventually, she comes to a few photographs where whatever was written on the back has been covered over with black marker. What's more interesting though, is the sticky film on those particular album pages isn't as sticky as some of the others. This was done recently, thinks Lydia, and certainly after the photographs had been placed in the album. Perhaps whoever put them in here didn't think anyone would ever take them out, or maybe they went in before her mother's name was changed by deed-pole. Maybe the marker is covering the name 'Margaret' on them.

Lydia takes a look at the time on the clock over the doorway; it's after midnight. She switches off the lamp and goes into the kitchen to get some water. Out of the corner of her eye she spots a laptop on a chair by the window, puts down the glass, and picks up the laptop. She places it carefully on the table and opens it. It's already turned on, and doesn't require a password either, so she immediately clicks on the email icon. Lydia isn't even sure what she's looking for, but on the off-chance that there's something in there that might prove anything, she has to have a look. She scrolls through everything in the inbox for the past few days, and nothing seems out of the ordinary. She goes through page after page of emails to and from family about upcoming trips, emails to co-workers about meetings. There is nothing suspicious at all. Then, Lydia decides to check the sent box. The very first email is to her mother, and the subject is 'Call me'. Lydia opens it immediately and reads:

'Lydia knows, doesn't she? How long can you keep this up?'

Her heart stops. She takes a moment to catch her breath, then re-reads the words to make sure she remembers them. It couldn't mean anything else, surely? There is something they are not telling her. She has to confront her aunt again.

26

Brian wakes to a text from his daughter with an update about the email she's found. He's excited that they're finally getting somewhere, but heartbroken at the same time. That email is proof that Barbara and her sister are definitely hiding something, but how the hell were they going to get anywhere if no-one was going to talk about it? His wife was literally willing to go to the grave with this secret.

He gets ready to leave the house, and walks the short distance to the hospital, remembering the day that they got the call to say Lydia was in there after collapsing on the street. He decides to call her, and gets through to her voicemail. He's worried all of a sudden, and decides to call Jane's landline instead. She picks up after two rings, sounds like she's in a good mood, but when she hears Brian's voice her tone changes.

'I had no idea Barbara was so bad, Brian. Do you want me to come over? You think it might help her?'

Brian feels himself being short with his sister-in-law. How could she act like this; feigning concern when she knows that all these lies are what's really the problem?

'Is Lydia there, Jane? I can't get through on her mobile.'

'Oh, you can't? That's weird.'

Brian listens as Jane calls Lydia's name up the stairs, and after a few seconds she tells Brian that she's probably gone for a walk with Jenny and the dog. She had mentioned that earlier, but Jane was probably in the shower when she left. Brian is already suspicious about Jane, but has no choice but to ask her to pass the message on to Lydia that he needs to speak to her. They hang up, he enters the hospital with an uneasy feeling in the pit of his stomach, and takes the lift to the third floor. Barbara is slightly more coherent at the moment, and has stopped crying as much, but she's been diagnosed with depression, and the psychiatrist says she's also displaying signs of post-traumatic stress disorder. Brian is pretty sure that even if he did confront her about the past, or told her what Lydia had found in the email, she wouldn't change her mind, or tell him anything. He loves her. He wants her to get better. But, she's also sort of a stranger to him at the moment.

'Where's Lydia?'

Barbara's eyes search around the room and look behind Brian, as if she is expecting Lydia to walk back into the room at any moment.

'She'll be here later on, or maybe tomorrow. She hasn't been feeling well. Tummy bug she thinks.'

Barbara looks guilty and nods slowly in understanding.

'She hates me. I don't blame her.'

'No-one hates you, darling. I promise. We just want you to get better.'

'You don't think it's my fault that Kate was taken?'

Brian doesn't know how to respond. What is he supposed to do here; point the finger, hoping that his wife will crack, and start telling him the truth? He's stuck. He needs Barbara alive and healthy, and can't risk her trying to kill herself again. He puts his hand on hers, tells her everything is going to be okay, and of course it isn't her fault Kate was taken. What more can he do for now?

'I'm going to go into the office for an hour or two, but I'll be back later, okay? Anything you need?'

Barbara shakes her head and closes her eyes.
'Tired' she mumbles.

27

Melvin has brought some things into the room for Kate and the baby. He seems really pleased and excited as he shows her each item before placing it on the dresser and chair. There are blankets, bottles, nappies, and a changing mat, as well as a few toys and books. She asks if she might be able to have her hands untied so she can take a proper look. Kate is genuinely excited to take a look; up to now, the room has been completely bare, apart from the bed clothes, bible, a few items of clothing, and a lamp. He hesitates, and Kate reassures him that she won't try anything. She laughs, and says that escape is the last thing on her mind, and there's nothing she wants more than to live here with him and Christine. The words seem entirely mad to Kate as she says them. What kind of idiot would believe that a nineteen-year-old girl would rather live with a deluded, murdering, rapist kidnapper, than at home with her wonderful family? But, Melvin seems relieved and happy to hear what she has said, nods, takes the key from around his neck, and unties her wrists. Kate thanks him as she rubs the parts of her arms where the metal cuffs rest; they're always slightly bruised and swollen. Then, she stands up and walks to the shopping bags and boxes on the floor. Kate always makes sure that her movements are gentle, slow, and she instinctively acts weaker than she really is. She doesn't want Melvin or Christine imagining that she is even capable of running or fighting. They want her weak and helpless, and she knows it. Christine joins them after a few minutes, and they all spend the next hour going through the baby stuff. Kate asks if there is any way they might consider allowing her a bit of time in the day where she isn't chained to the bed, so she can walk around. She's found a section in one of the books that says it's important to take gentle exercise throughout pregnancy, and women who stay active have less chance of complications during birth. Melvin's ears prick at the mention of complications, and he stares at the book for a few seconds, looking puzzled, then nods slowly, and tells Kate he thinks she should exercise, and she will have an hour every day to do whatever she likes, once she stays in this room, of course. Kate is visibly excited.

'I know exactly what I can do! Yoga and… just even walking around the room will be so good for me and the baby. Keep the circulation going and everything.'

Kate is pleased with this outcome and progress; she needs to prove that they can trust her without being chained up all the time, and being able to walk around the room will be amazing. Melvin and Christine go downstairs to sort out dinner, and although she is chained again, Kate is allowed to keep the three books with her. She's never been keener to read in her life; this is the first thing besides the bible she has read in nearly six months.

28

Jared gets into his car and texts Lydia to see if she's free for a chat. He has been thinking about her non-stop since the last time they were together, and he's angry with himself for hurting her like that. She looked so broken that morning. He couldn't be without her now, no matter how complicated things had become. But, he worries that she won't trust him again after this; he had let her down just like everyone else had, but would do everything in his power to make it up to her. Lydia doesn't respond to the text, and he knows that if he doesn't speak to her now, he won't get the chance to until tonight, so he decides to call her. But Lydia doesn't see the call coming through; she's boarding a plane. Her aunt had looked right through her this morning when she confronted her about the email. It was remarkable. She'd acted like Lydia had made it all up, and simply pushed past her to make some coffee. It was actually kind of scary. How could she go from being so warm and fun the night before, to this utter coldness? When Lydia had tried to show her what she'd seen on the laptop, Jane has almost hissed at her to leave it alone. Lydia had gone upstairs, Jane followed, and said she should probably leave. So, Lydia found herself getting into a taxi and going back to the airport. She felt like a failure; she had barely been in Florida twenty-four hours and now had to return home, empty-handed. But she was desperate to see Jared and her dad, and felt that she had at least found something in the email that confirmed her mum was lying, and Jane knew about it. Lydia had no idea what her mother was trying to hide, exactly. How bad could it be? Did she kill someone? Did someone hurt her?

How could it be connected to Kate's disappearance, and why would her mother keep this information away from police and her own family? It just wasn't adding up. Lydia had been awake for most of the night at Jane's. In fact, she hasn't slept properly in days. She quickly texts her dad and Jared to say she's okay, and will be back in London in eight hours or so, and as soon as the plane leaves the runway, she's asleep. In her dream, Kate is sitting next to her on the plane, resting her head on her shoulder. She tells her that everything is going to be alright because she has a plan, and they will be together again. Lydia wakes just as the plane is landing, and ten minutes later, walks through passport control and baggage collection in a daze. As she's waiting for her suitcase to appear she calls Jared, and tells him about what happened, and the email she found on her aunt's computer. She really wants to see him tonight, but has to speak to her parents first. Jared's surprised at how upbeat and energetic she sounds. She's been through so much over the past six months; her sister's abduction, her mother's breakdown and attempted suicide, and then he wasn't there for her when he should've been. He apologises, and she can hear in his voice that he's suffering too. Lydia feels more mature than she ever has before. She reassures Jared that she's okay and says she'll speak to him later. Then she calls her dad, and tells him she'll be home in an hour or so, depending on traffic. She needs to talk to him. Brian sounds like he's in a daze when he picks up the phone, but when he hears his daughter's voice, he jumps into action. He has to get the place in order before she gets back, and sober up from the whisky he's been downing.

An hour and twenty minutes later, Lydia is in a taxi

driving past Hampstead Heath train station, when she sees Ida coming out of the newsagents across the road. The car slows to allow a few kids to cross at the pedestrian crossing, and Lydia waves and catches her eye. Ida initially looks surprised to see her, and then extremely happy; she makes her way towards the car and Lydia asks the driver to stop. She apologises, and explains that the lady is a friend that she urgently needs to speak to. He smiles, tells her it's not a problem, and pulls over immediately. Lydia opens the door, and the first thing Ida says is that she needs to speak to her immediately. Lydia pays the fare, thanks the friendly driver, and hops out onto the pavement, pulling her suitcase behind her.

'Can we go to my house now? I'm sorry to do this Lydia it's just...'

Lydia sees Ida's face is a shade of grey, and her eyes are bloodshot. She had always looked so healthy and relaxed, but today she looks ill and sad.

'Of course. What's wrong? Are you alright Ida?'

Ida forces a little smile, and puts a reassuring, firm hand on Lydia's arm.

'My sweet girl. I'm okay. Don't worry about me. I'm old!'

She gives a little laugh, but Lydia isn't buying it; it's obvious that Ida is not good. She looks frail and troubled.

'Is it Kate? Do you know something? Have you had another vision?'

'Let's just get to mine and have a cup of tea and I'll tell you everything okay?'

When they arrive at Ida's house, Lydia immediately notices that it looks and smells different. It is a beautiful house, and usually gleaming and airy. But the front curtains are drawn, the reception room is cloaked in darkness, and there is a musty smell in the air. It's also freezing and Lydia starts to shiver as she walks down the hallway into the kitchen where Ida is putting the kettle on. Even Angel seems unlike her usual self, and doesn't even bother to leave her bed on the back of the Aga to greet Lydia as she usually does.

'Ida, I hope you don't mind me saying but...'

'I know. I know. The place is a mess! I'm sorry. I don't know why I've let it get so bad. Oh, and I've turned the heating on so it should be warming up soon. Sorry about that.'

Lydia feels a wave of emotion. Ida has been so good to Lydia, and so kind these past six months, and she's obviously struggling herself, right now. It breaks Lydia's heart to see.

'Why don't you let me help? I'd really love to, and we can have this place back to its usual in no time!'

Ida stops what she's doing and nods gently. A smile appears on her face and lights up her eyes. Lydia is such a generous soul, Ida thinks; there's nothing selfish or greedy about her. She's one of those rare people who really sees others as they are, and Ida appreciates that. Even now, after everything she's going through, she's concerned about this house being messy and wants to help. Ida hands her a blue mug and tells her it's hot, and to be careful.

'We have things to do first, alright? But thank you for your very kind offer. It would be nice to have some help.'

Lydia assumes that they are going to go out to the adjoining conservatory where they usually have their sessions, but Ida motions to two armchairs in the kitchen next to the window, instead.

She doesn't want to tell Lydia, and risk scaring her, but the conservatory is no longer a place where Ida feels comfortable. She's had so many hellish visions out there over the past month or so, and no matter what she does, she can't clear the energy. She's tried sage, crystals, asking her angels and guides to help, but nothing is working. Whatever force is here, is staying, for a while at least, and Ida has decided to accept it. Because, however dark and debilitating it is; it's guiding her to Kate, and the other girl.

Lydia sits in one armchair, sipping her tea, and Ida sits in the other. She isn't sure why, but Lydia feels strangely euphoric today. There's something inside of her that truly believes everything is going to work out, and that good is going to overcome evil. She believes Kate is alive and will come home, the mystery of her mother's life is going to come into the light, and she and Jared will work out, too.

'My heart feels strong Ida.' she finds herself suddenly saying. Ida nods, smiles at her, and takes a sip from her mug, before placing it on the small wooden table in front of her. Angel suddenly appears, and rubs herself against Lydia's legs.

'That cat can sense your strength' Ida says with a gentle laugh.

'She's always liked you more than the average person that comes in here, you know?'

'Has she?'

Lydia smiles and strokes Angel. The cat's white fur seems to catch the bright grey light from the window, making her almost glow in a magical way. Lydia and Ida spend a few minutes admiring her, and her bright coat, before Ida clears her throat, and decides to broach the subject of Kate. She tells Lydia about the extreme visions she's been having, and how it's been unlike anything she's ever experienced before. She tells her about the other girl and how she looks just like Kate with the same long dark hair and big eyes. Ida believes that this other girl is another victim that may have been taken before Kate, or even at the same time, and she was murdered. Ida seems pained by what she's telling Lydia, and says that she doesn't want to go into too much detail, but the murder scene in her visions is bloody and brutal... She can also see that this other girl was kept in the same place as Kate.

'If there is another girl missing out there that looks like Kate, maybe that could lead to your sister.'

It's a lot for Lydia to take in; her mind is swimming with all that she has just heard, and she's trying to piece it together, along with the information about her mother's true identity, and this secret group.

'Do you think that maybe my mum was part of something like... like... an evil cult, and she escaped, but these people came after her? Maybe they kill young girls as a kind of sacrifice or something... or they want revenge against my mum, so they took Kate? And this other girl is in a similar situation?'

Lydia is on her feet now, and slowly walking around the dimly-lit kitchen. A picture is forming in her head about what Ida's visions could mean. But this murdered girl doesn't make sense. Why would they kill her, but keep Kate alive? Assuming Kate is alive. Ida listens to Lydia in quiet contemplation; she doesn't know what else to say to the poor girl, but reiterates that she strongly feels this dead girl was kept in the same place as Kate, and if they can find her, or have any information about her at all, it might lead them to Kate.

After half an hour or so, Lydia hugs Ida, and tells her she has to go, but will talk to her soon.

'I've got someone I think might know about this other girl. I'll let you know, okay? Stay warm, and thank you Ida! You are a true friend. Thank you!'

Lydia feels bad leaving Ida alone, but she has to speak to her dad and Jared about this new information. She breaks into a jog as she makes her way down Pond Street, and around the corner towards Hepburn House on East Heath Road.

29

At home, Lydia fills her dad in on everything that's happened. He looks disturbed when he hears about Ida's visions about the other murdered girl. If this is true, and Ida really is seeing the place where Kate is being held captive, then the people that have her are murderers. Brian is really struggling to get to grips with everything that's going on. What use was this information if they have no idea where to start looking? Lydia reassures him; she has been in touch with Detective McCarthy again, and he's said he will find some time to meet with her over the next day or two.

'We need to start looking at other missing girls online, Dad. Anyone that looks like Kate could be the girl that Ida's seen in her visions. They could lead us to her!'

Brian listens to Lydia, but can feel his heart sinking in his chest. He is a practical, rational thinker, and has zero experience or faith in paranormal activity or psychics. He doesn't want to upset his daughter, but the more he thinks about it, the more likely it seems that Ida is just a mad woman, or a con artist who makes her money from duping sad, desperate people like Lydia into thinking their missing or dead loved ones are still out there. Lydia senses the shift in him. He's not even looking at her directly in the eye anymore; it's like he's looking through her. She suddenly realises how awful he looks; like he hasn't slept at all. She feels a small wave of guilt, sits on the sofa opposite, and asks how her mum is, and what's happened at the hospital. Lydia listens as he tells her they are keeping her mum in the psychiatric ward for the moment, and she's been prescribed all sorts of things like mood stabilizers. The doctor told him that she said she had been suicidal for years. Lydia refuses to believe it, and shakes her head repeatedly. Why would her mother say such a thing? That would mean she had been hiding and lying to the whole family all this time; pretending that everything was fine when inside she wanted to die? How is that even possible?

'Dad, I don't know what Mum has gone through, but it's beginning to feel like we don't know her at all. I think whatever she is running from, and whatever she was involved with is darker than we can even imagine.'

Lydia waits for her father to respond to the weight of what she's just said, but he's not really listening. He just nods slowly, and picks up his phone. Lydia accepts that the conversation is over, for now, and decides to make a healthy meal for both of them. She starts to peel some vegetables she spots in a cardboard box on the floor. Her mum subscribes to one of those fancy online companies what deliver organic vegetable boxes every week, and for the first time Lydia is grateful for it. She announces what she's cooking to her dad, but he's staring vacantly at the muted television. Forty minutes later, Lydia produces a delicious meal of sautéed leek and mushrooms, cubed, roasted potatoes with herbs, and baked Alaskan red salmon she found in the freezer. She's afraid her dad won't eat it because he looks so disinterested, but he devours every bite and asks for seconds. Lydia is in the middle of serving him some more when a text comes through from Jared saying he is parked down the road. She walks into the living room to tell her dad she needs to go out, but finds him fast asleep on the sofa with Molly curled up behind his legs. She tells the dog to stay, puts the plate of food back in the oven so it stays warm, and goes straight out the front door, texting Jared to say she's on her way. He texts back to say he's in the car park on the way towards the heath station.

The pair embrace as soon as Lydia gets into the car. Jared immediately starts apologising about his behaviour, and Lydia tells him to forget it; he is forgiven. She quickly tells him about what happened with Ida, and that she needs his help tracking down any missing girls that look like Kate in the past few years. Lydia isn't sure how many years back they should go. It sounds like a long shot, now that she's explaining her theory to an actual expert in this area, and she can feel her face flush, but Jared is totally on board and encouraging. He listens to everything she has to say and says he'll start looking immediately; he has access to details and photographs of everyone who has been reported missing in the UK for the past fifty years or so, and he reassures Lydia that he will do everything in his power to find this other girl, if she exists. Lydia kisses him goodbye, whispers that she loves him, and Jared tells her that he won't let her down again. She opens the car door and smiles back at him.

'Lyds? Just so you know... if Kate's case is reopened we will have to be extra careful... you know... with 'us'. Okay?'

Lydia nods in understanding and tells him not to worry. She walks briskly home and breathes in the cold evening air; it catches her throat and almost burns her nostrils. She had barely noticed winter tightening its grip on the city over the past few weeks, and tonight, she hopes that wherever her sister was,

30

For the past week, Kate's plan to escape has seemed more reality than fantasy, but she needs to execute her plan before it's too late, or pregnancy makes it too difficult. She's figured out that she's probably been pregnant for about four or five months now. She's gained weight, feels pretty strong, and has been using the time when she's untied to do yoga on the woven floor mat, as well as gentle jogging on the spot. Melvin doesn't really like the jogging; it causes too much noise on the wooden floors, and he tells her to just walk around the room and do some stretches, instead. But Kate wants to make sure that if it comes to it, and she has to run from this house, she's as fast as she can be, so whenever she thinks Melvin is outside with the dogs or gone somewhere else, she jogs. She is also enjoying the ability to see out from the bedroom window every day; a small but important privilege she now appreciates very much.

Tonight, Melvin has gone on an impromptu trip into town, and Christine has been up in Kate's room. The pair have been talking and snacking on crisps that Christine found on the top shelf in the pantry. Kate is constantly hungry these days and her captors seem to delight in feeding her up; as if every mouthful is going straight to the baby, ensuring he will be as healthy as possible. Christine refuses any more of the crisps and hands the packet to Kate with a wink. Kate gets into bed and covers herself up with the blankets, she's starting to doze off as she listens to Christine speak about the ranch days, when she first realised Melvin was going to ask her to marry him, and how devastating it was after they were married and realised she couldn't get pregnant. Melvin had seen this as further evidence that Margaret was the one who was supposed to carry his child, and Christine was full of shame. Suddenly, they hear a noise that sounds like a loud bang at the front door. Kate's eyes open widely, and she stares at Christine, who goes to peek out the window. But, she can't see anything, and hurries downstairs to investigate. Kate smiles to herself; Christine has forgotten to tie her hands up again. If she can get away with it for the remainder of the evening, they might go to bed and leave her untied. This is exactly the kind of scenario she had hoped for when she asked them to consider untying her for longer periods of time.

Downstairs, Christine opens the front door to a grumpy Melvin. He had forgotten his keys and asks why it took so long for her to let him in. She explains that she was just checking on Kate upstairs, and he nods reluctantly in understanding, then walks into the kitchen, and points out that dinner hasn't even been started. Christine hurries to turn the oven on, pulling her apron from the back of the door; she knows she needs to make dinner as quickly as possible; she's still afraid of Melvin's temper, although it's been weeks since he's hit her, or shouted that much. She has almost forgotten Kate upstairs.

About an hour before Melvin and Christine go to bed, it's Melvin who pops his head around the door and asks Kate if she needs the bathroom. She is ready for this, and with her arms firmly hidden under the blankets, she tells him that she'll be okay until morning, and Christine took her to the bathroom earlier. She tells him she's exhausted and just needs to sleep, he seems satisfied with that, and closes the door quietly, telling

Kate to sleep well, and call out if she feels unwell or needs anything. He's been saying this for the past couple of weeks; asking her if she needs anything and expressing his concern for her well-being. Kate noticed the shock on Christine's face when he said it in front of her for the first time. It was more than likely jealousy; Kate believed that Christine was just as twisted and brainwashed as her sick husband, and she craved his attention and approval, even after all he had put her through. God knows what happened to Christine in the past, or what horrors she had seen that messed with her mind, Kate thinks to herself. She had been born into the cult. At least Kate's mother was only involved for a couple of years before she escaped, but Christine knew nothing else.

To an outsider, it might seem like Melvin genuinely cares for Kate's well-being. He doesn't look like a kidnapper, rapist, or murderer when he enquires about how she's feeling, or brings her food on a tray. But Kate knows what he is, and she also knows that this kindness isn't really meant for her; it's meant for the baby she's carrying that he believes is some sort of blessed and divine hero; his connection to God and heaven. When the baby is born she will be disposable to Melvin. She has to remember that. Tonight, she is going to try to get out of here.

A little while later, Christine is in the laundry room downstairs when she hears Melvin outside in the hallway. She knows he doesn't know she's in there because he's muttering to himself in the way that he does sometimes when he believes he's alone. Sometimes Christine hears it while he's in the bath or if she suddenly walks into the room. She smiles to herself, and shakes her head, trying to make out what he's saying. Then, she hears him pull out the small stool next to the hall table, and suddenly he's talking to someone on the phone out there, almost in a whisper. Christine tiptoes to the door and strains to hear what he's saying, but can only make out a few words. He seems to be quite angry with whoever is at the end of the line, and warns them that they better be giving him the correct information and not making a mistake. She hears him spit out 'You better realise what's at stake here.' before hanging up. He then swears much more loudly and a second later asks God to forgive him, and wash away his sins and filthy tongue. Christine hears the stool scrape the floor and her heart jumps. She quickly tiptoes back to the other side of the laundry room and picks up some pillow cases. A few seconds later, Melvin pushes the door open, and glares at her from the doorway. He must have heard her.

'What are you doing?' he snaps.

He walks into the room and examines the pile of laundry she's folding.

'Just these sheets and towels. Is there anything you'd like me to wash for you? I was going to...'

But before she can finish, she feels a hard burn against her cheek. Her whole body responds to the sensation, and she lets out a cry.

'Shut up, you stupid bitch.'

He's laughing now and his eyes are alight. It's all too familiar to Christine; Melvin gets angry and frustrated, and takes it out on her, beats her until she begs for his forgiveness, and then he apologises. The cycle has been like this for as long as she can remember, but it doesn't get easier. She still hopes that one day he will stop, and learn to respect her more. Maybe one day he will see how devoted she is, and that she doesn't

109

mean to upset him. Melvin asks if she heard what he was saying on the telephone, and Christine stares back blankly at him; her mouth open in shock and fear. She doesn't want to lie, but also doesn't want to make this worse for herself. Her silence infuriates him. He lunges forward, and pushes her hard towards the fridge freezer. She hits it, then falls to the floor, and stays down as he hovers over her. Spittle is starting to build up in the front of his mouth, and glistens on his dry, cracked lips. He roars at her to get up, but just as Christine is finding her feet, he pushes her again, and when she hits the wall and slumps to the ground this time, he grabs a fistful of her hair and pulls her head back viciously.

'Look at me!' he almost growls at her.

'Look at me, I said!'

Christine's whole body is shaking. All she can feel is the pain in her right shoulder and elbow where she's hit the fridge door handle, and the hot stinging on her face. She uses every ounce of strength she has to look him in the eye, and tells him she's very sorry to upset him, and won't do it again. Melvin's smile exposes his bad teeth, and from this angle Christine can see right up his huge, hairy nostrils. He leans forward a few inches and pulls her head back even more, so her face is directly beneath his. Then, he spits at her. It lands right in her left eye, and he laughs as she blinks on reflex. He enjoys this; humiliating Christine, making her feel small and afraid, and by default making himself feel strong and big. He spits again, this time getting Christine in the other eye.

'Stupid woman.'

He lets go of her and walks towards the door.

'Wash your filthy face. I'm going to bed.'

It takes about ten minutes for Christine to compose herself. She cries into some of the damp sheets to drown out the sounds, and when she feels a little bit better, she splashes some water on her face, and takes a few deep breaths.

'Thank you, God, for making it quick this time. Please forgive me for my sins.'

Upstairs, Kate is also praying. Not for herself and her family like she usually does, but for Christine. As twisted as the situation is, she can still see that she has been victimised too. She wonders if Christine's face will be bruised badly tomorrow, and knows that she probably won't come into the room now, because she will be too embarrassed. She listens as Melvin goes into the bathroom first, then into their bedroom, and fifteen minutes later, Christine joins him. At least forty minutes pass, and Kate hopes they're both asleep by now.

The moon is almost full tonight, and Kate can see its familiar, comforting light seep in through a crack in the curtains as she goes over the plan in her mind. She has been practising walking this room many times, and knows which floorboards creak, and how to spread her weight slowly and evenly on them. She thinks that it would take Melvin at least twenty seconds or more to go from his room across the landing to her bedroom door, unlock it, and come inside. If they did hear her moving around, she would have enough time to get back into bed and hide. The dangerous bit, the first hurdle, is getting the bedroom door unlocked without a key. But Kate has already planned for this; she has a small flat piece of metal in her hand that she pulled from the lampshade, and she's gripping it tightly now.

The door has what she can only guess is an emergency hinge that actually turns the lock and opens the door. When Kate first saw it a few weeks ago, it seemed too good to be true. But when she tried to turn it with the piece of metal, it slowly moved, and she could hear the metal parts turn inside. She didn't want to turn it fully, in case she couldn't turn it back again; that would risk Melvin knowing what she had done, or at least becoming suspicious of her, and he might have changed the lock and tied her up all the time again. But now, she had to turn it as much as she could, and hopefully get out of this room.

The moonlight illuminates everything, and Kate sees its help as further evidence that tonight is the night. The moon is on her and her baby's side. Kate listens in the darkness for any sound from the house. There's nothing. She thinks about the next steps once the door is opened. It was pretty much all guess work. For all she knows, Melvin might sleep with the keys around his neck, and every door and window might be locked tightly. There might even be some kind of alarm system or security lights somewhere, not to mention how impossible it would be getting past the dogs and gates if she actually makes it outside. She says a quick prayer, and touches her stomach gently.

'Please, please let me get out of here.'

The hinge turns, and when the lock is released it makes a small click that seems loud in the dark stillness. Kate waits for a few seconds before testing the door to see how quietly she can move it towards her. It moves silently and easily, and she uses both hands to control it. When it's open, she very carefully places one foot in front, and eases it onto the floor. It creaks slightly and Kate stops. She doesn't know the sounds of every floorboard in the hall, although she knows that the stairs are creaky and there is a rail that she has seen going down one side. She gently eases her left foot down next to her right, until she's standing in between her bedroom and the bathroom. There is moonlight in the small landing and she can see Melvin and Christine's bedroom door, about fifteen feet away. Kate looks at it, and is filled with anger at them both, and a determination to get away from this place, forever. She turns to the stairs in front of her, and makes her way to the first step. Suddenly, she hears something; it's movement from their bedroom; the sound of heavy feet on the ground. Melvin. Kate turns, and quickly travels the few steps back to her bedroom. She's shaking. She closes the door behind her, but it won't click shut because she has turned the safety key. It's too late. Melvin opens his bedroom door and Kate can hear him walking towards her. Her heart sinks. She's holding the door shut, and wonders if she should just let it go and jump back into bed. Maybe he would believe it just broke on its own, somehow? Before she can make a decision, she hears another sound; the bathroom door. She breathes out quickly and reaches into her right sock for the flat metal piece. Her eyes have adjusted to the dark, and it's easier this time. In a few seconds, the door is locked again, Kate tiptoes to her bed, and climbs under the covers. She tries to make her breathing return to normal, but her heart is beating so fast and strongly that she can almost hear it. Then, Melvin is at the door. Kate hears the key in the lock, and shuts her eyes tightly.

31

As if Lydia knows what's going on in her sister's world, she lies awake too, and watches as the clock turns 3.00AM. Then, she falls into a light, fitful sleep where she's following Kate through a crowd, but keeps losing sight of her. Lydia wakes again at 7.00AM drenched in sweat, and exhausted. She pulls on a hoody over her striped pyjamas, and goes downstairs to make some coffee. Molly scratches at the door to come into the kitchen, and Lydia bends down to stroke her golden head. She barks, and walks over to where her lead hangs on a hook by the back door. Lydia tries to quieten the dog, and opens the door for her in case she needs to pee, but Molly sniffs at the morning air and rejects the idea. Lydia dares not to even mention the 'W' word (walkies) in case Molly starts to bark with excitement. She doesn't want to wake her dad. But when she discovers that they are out of coffee, even the instant stuff, she tells Molly that she's a lucky dog, and grabs her coat, wellies, and the dog lead. She needs caffeine today, full stop.

Ten minutes later, Kate and Molly are walking through the village when Lydia realises that nowhere is going to be open this early. How did she not think of that? She almost laughs at herself. Here she is, in a strange outfit, with a hyperactive dog, sniffing around the village like a coffee addict. Then, she remembers seeing a twenty-four-hour newsagent on the other side of the hospital, and decides to check it out. She walks past the huge building, and thinks how strange it is that her mother is inside right this second, lying there, drugged up. Life is so bizarre. She takes a little side lane off Pond Street that she thinks will lead to the newsagent she has in mind, and notices a man is sitting on the bench about half way up the lane. Suddenly, Lydia feels uncomfortable; the man is staring at her, and there's no-one else around. Molly senses it too, and slows her bouncy trot down to a cautious walk, glancing up at Lydia a few times. He's wearing a long green thing that looks like overalls or some kind of workman's uniform. He also has a small navy fisherman's hat on his head, and large, black laced-up boots that are covered in dust, or dried mud. Lydia can see that he's looking right at her. As she gets closer, she can see his features more clearly; a large, overhanging brow, thick dark eyebrows, and very large eyes. Lydia is feeling uneasy, but she continues to walk, reasoning that she doesn't feel like herself anyway, and is probably just freaked out because of everything that's been going on and what she's going through, as well as jet-lag and the awful night's sleep she had at her aunt's. When she is about ten feet away from him, the man slowly stands up, as if he's stiff or in pain. Lydia keeps her eyes ahead, and a thought enters her mind: maybe he is a patient at the hospital. She passes, and glances in his direction, then gently calls 'Come on, good girl' to Molly. Lydia is doing everything she can to remain calm, when everything in her body is telling her to run. She gets to the top of the path, just before the newsagent's, and stops for a moment to reach into her coat pocket for her phone. Suddenly, she feels hands on her. She shrieks with fright and Molly barks. It's him.

32

Jared is working from home today. He sleepily makes his way downstairs, pops a couple of slices of seeded bread into the toaster, puts the kettle on for coffee, and opens his laptop to log into the system. He had made a start last night when he got in, but still hasn't come across any missing young women that look like the Stone twins. Jared hasn't really told many people this, but his grandmother, Sally was a psychic medium, so Ida's visions aren't so crazy to him. He remembers being a little kid and watching as ladies came and went from his grandma's house, trying to get in touch with loved ones who had passed away, or asking what their future might hold. On the days that he and his sister, Antionette were with their grandma, they would spend most of the time begging her to teach them how to tell the future, and asking about the clients that came to see her. She would smile at them, her brown eyes twinkling, and tell them it was a secret. But Jared was obsessed, and still practised as much as he could. He tried it on his parents and his sister, his friends at school, and was constantly guessing what would happen; if it would rain, what they would be having for dinner, what someone's name was. When he got to about ten years old he stopped seeing his grandma as much because his parents divorced and his mom moved out of town, so they only saw Grandma when their dad brought them to see her on the occasional weekend. When Lydia told him about Ida she seemed so cautious; like he was going to laugh, or think less of her for believing in all that stuff. But he found it fascinating, and assuming Ida was genuine, there just might be something in all these visions she's been having that could guide them to Kate.

He skims through photographs of girls from cases; some that he's familiar with, or worked on, and some that are new to him. The toast pops, he goes to butter it, and makes some coffee afterwards, then he makes his way back to the table, munching on the toast, and continues to scroll through photos of missing girls. Any brunettes he comes across, or anyone that even has similar features to the twins gets saved to a folder named 'For Lydia'. He figures that some of these photographs might not accurately show the girls' hair or could be taken years before they went missing, or even before they dyed it. He didn't want to miss anything, or let Lydia down. All of a sudden, Jared comes to Melanie Latter's file, and his eyes open in amazement. He looks away for a moment then takes another look at the screen. It's quite remarkable. She could easily be Kate and Lydia's sister. She has the same dark eyes and long, dark hair. Even their jawlines were identical. He reads the date on Melanie's file. She was fifteen when she went missing in 2015, almost a year before Kate, and the last anyone saw of her was when she stormed out of a teenage disco after having an argument with friends. Jared scrolls through, looking for details on the location, and sees that Melanie went missing in Banbury, Oxfordshire. Her mobile phone was found in a ditch on the A361 which is the opposite direction of her home, so, either someone picked her up in a car, and threw it from the window as they drove, or they found her there, and for whatever reason her phone fell out of her coat or bag, or was purposefully left in the ditch. Jared reads the entire file and starts trying to piece things together. If this is the girl from Ida's visions, and she was held in the same place that Kate was, then that could be close to Banbury. He needed to show this photograph to Ida as soon as possible. It was also worth drawing Detective McCarthy's attention to the findings. It was his case after all, and although it hasn't been an active investigation for months now, Jared doesn't want to upset anyone, and look like he is going behind their backs. He picks up the phone to call Lydia. There's no answer, and he leaves a message asking her to call him back immediately.

Lydia is walking behind the strange man and trying to keep Molly quiet. As soon as she looked him in the eye, close up, she recognised him; it was the same man who had stood outside the house looking for 'Margaret' all those months ago. At that time, Lydia had no idea that name was significant; she thought he was just some mentally ill, or homeless man. He had scared her then, and he scared her today. He said he knew her mother, and Lydia had backed away from him, and was about to run away, but then he said something else that captured her attention completely. He told her that if she wanted to see her sister again, she should follow him. So, she did. What else could she do? This was it; this weird man knew something, and Lydia had to find out what it was. She takes the phone from her pocket to text Jared, but as soon as she starts to type, the battery dies.

'Shit. Shit. Shit.'

She's whispering, but the man seems to hear and looks back at her angrily.

'Don't call anyone, alright? That's important!'

He stops walking, and glares at her. Lydia nods furiously; she doesn't want him to leave, she needs to see and hear the truth, and has to be brave for her sister. They continue to walk, and somewhere between Hampstead and Gospel Oak, the man turns down a street and points ahead at some terraced houses.

'Just round the back, here.'

Lydia takes a deep breath, and continues to follow him. Molly is walking obediently next to her, and Lydia sees her obedience as a sign that this man isn't dangerous. They walk down a very narrow alley-way between the terraced houses, and come out in what looks like an old scrapyard of some kind. Lydia looks around, and is relieved to see a young woman with two small children coming out of one of the front doors. She's buttoning their coats, and making sure their hats are on their heads properly. Lydia wants the woman to see her, and stops for a moment to look in her direction. One of the children, the little boy, sees her first, and waves, then his mother looks up and smiles, too. They may be witnesses if no-one sees her again, Lydia thinks. The man is standing outside a four-story grey building now, that looks like a block of flats. There's some sort of writing on a sign over the front door that makes Lydia think it must be a halfway house, or some other kind of charity or care home; it's the most depressing thing she's seen in a long time; the windows are tiny, and there's rubbish strewn all over the concrete ground at the front of the building. There's the remnants of a bicycle tied to bike stand without wheels, a seat, or chain. This place couldn't be more dissimilar to the street that Lydia and her family live on, and yet it's only a fifteen-minute walk away. The air seems heavy and dirty, and there isn't a green, living thing to be seen anywhere around the place. The man enters a code into a key pad on the door and he holds it open for Lydia to follow. He motions for her to stay by the door, and puts a dirty finger to his lips to let her know to be quiet. His eyes are still angry, and Lydia nods in agreement, slowly reaching down to reassure Molly with a head stroke, as she watches the man pop his head around the corner and tell someone he needs to use the lift. They must need to open it for him; a security measure, Lydia assumes. A few moments later, they are inside the elevator, and travelling up. The doors ping open on the fourth floor, and by that time, Lydia has figured out he wants to get her in the elevator instead of taking the stairs, because that way she won't be seen by the person downstairs in the reception, or maybe even a security camera. It slowly occurs to her that this isn't a very good sign. But it feels like it's too late. She's here now. Then, another thought occurs to Lydia that quickly replaces all others; what if Kate is here?

34

Jared purposefully bumps into McCarthy in the kitchen, and tells him he's come across a missing girl file from 2015, and the girl looks remarkably like Kate Stone. McCarthy looks exhausted, and doesn't seem like he wants to engage in conversation, so Jared changes the subject, and asks about a couple of other active cases he's working on. McCarthy seems distracted and tells Jared he'll see him later. But Jared can't just leave it there.

'Hey, I'm going to send you a pic of that missing girl, the one who looks like Kate Stone. The similarity is crazy!'

McCarthy nods and waves as he leaves the break room with his coffee mug; he has been up all night with his daughter Elsa who has chickenpox. Today, of all days, he is not on Jared's wavelength. But, ten minutes later, Jared sends an email to him with a photograph of Kate Stone attached, and next to it, a photo of Melanie Latter. McCarthy has to take a second look, and a third. It really is amazing how alike the two girls are. He looks around, and calls out to one of his favourite colleagues, DCI Margo Maclaren, who happens to be walking past his office. She walks in, and McCarthy asks if she thinks the two girls look alike, and she responds asking if they are the Stone twins. When McCarthy says they are not known to be related, but both girls are missing, she looks shocked, and peers at the screen for a few seconds before announcing that she would bet quite a lot of money that they are sisters, or at least first cousins.

'You're not a betting woman are you, DCI Maclaren?' McCarthy teases.

'I most certainly am not! But even I would put a few quid on those two being related.'

Her phone rings and she winks at McCarthy before as she answers it, and leaves the office. McCarthy continues to stare at the screen. Jared pops his head around the door a few minutes later to see what McCarthy thinks. He is prepared for another cold shoulder, but is pleased to see that his plan is working, and McCarthy is taking this seriously.

'What led you to this, by the way, Jared? We haven't looked at the Stone case for ages now.'

Jared already knows that he can't mention any sort of relationship with Lydia, never mind a psychic in Hampstead who has been having visions telling him to look at old files of missing girls.

'Just tidying up some old cases, and it caught my eye really, mate.'

McCarthy nods and thanks him. He doesn't have time today, but he will get someone to look into this.

Back at his desk, Jared makes a plan. The first thing they need to do is cross-reference the photograph of Melanie with Ida's visions, then Lydia needs to go to McCarthy independently and tell him what the psychic told her. Then, hopefully Jared can legitimately add Kate Stone back on to his active list, and work on it alongside his other cases. He picks up his phone and texts Lydia. It's after 9AM, and unlike her not to get back to him. Perhaps she's had a bad night's sleep, he thinks.

35

Lydia and Molly are inside the man's bedsit. The place stinks, and Lydia spots an open tin of baked beans on its side, and covered in green mould on top of an overflowing bin. He tells her to sit down. Lydia nods, and diligently sits on the arm of the brown leatherette sofa. The man sits on the small, single bed across the room.

'What's your name?'

He shakes his head.

'No names. I know where your sister is, and I know who has her. I know all of the secrets of your family.'

Lydia is speechless. She waits for him to continue, and notices his face looks sad, and almost contemplative.

'How do you know my family, my mother? Is it from...?

'The ranch? From Texas? Sure is.'

Lydia's eyes widen. She feels the urge to stand up and go over to him.

'Tell me! Please, tell me where Kate is? Do they have her?'

He looks back at her and seems suddenly entertained at her desperate pleas. His eyes are brighter now, and he starts to laugh. His laughter grows, and soon he is rocking back and forth with the weight of it. Lydia asks him again:

'Please, tell me how I can get to my sister.'

He stands up, and walks to the counter; there's a microwave, lots of old food wrappers, and a few dirty cups on it. On top of the microwave are lots of papers and envelopes. With his dirty fingers, the man pulls a photograph out, and looks at it, then, he turns to Lydia and holds it out for her to see. She gets up and moves closer to him. She doesn't recognise anyone in the photograph; it's a family with two sons. They look pretty happy.

'What does this have to do with my sister? Who are they?'

He takes a step back, and indignantly tells her that is his family.

'They took my sons! Just like they took your sister.'

Lydia is confused, and asks him once again who took her sister. He stares back at her, eyes glazed, then he begins to cry and tells her that his parents joined a ranch in Colorado when he was twelve, and he lived there until he was thirty-seven. He had two boys and a wife, but she died in a car accident while he was away on another ranch in Texas. He met Margaret and her sister Cassie when he was there, and they helped him through the heartache of losing his wife and being separated from his sons. Lydia works out that Cassie is actually her Aunt Jane. They must have both changed their names when they left the ranch. Why hadn't she thought of that before? Lydia is nodding in encouragement, and finding it hard to stop herself from hurrying him to finish the story. He tells her that her mother and her sister had lost both of their parents. Their father had some kind of disease and their mother had died in mysterious circumstances while she was away from them. He remembers hearing that, and just knowing that he wasn't safe, and his sons weren't either. He already knew the violence and cruelty that existed in the church, and he knew for certain that it was not part of God's plan. Lydia interrupts him. She can't bear it anymore, and bursts into tears. She lunges forward and grabs his hands. Her body is almost collapsing as she sobs. Molly barks, and jumps up on her, trying to reassure her.

'Please, tell me where my sister is. Please!'

The man stops speaking, pushes her away gently, and takes a couple of shuffling steps back until he's sitting on the bed again.

'There is a man who was the son of the leader of the group. We're talking in charge of thousands of the group's members. Melvin Todd was his name, he was part of his father, Joseph Todd's prophecy, where Melvin would have a baby with a beautiful dark-haired young woman, and that baby would be a boy and the next saviour of the world. He wanted your mother to be that mother to that baby y'see and... I helped her escape. I believe he's the one who's got your sister, and by finding him, you'll find her.'

Lydia asks him again to tell her his name. He takes a moment before whispering:

'Dale. Dale Adams'

Lydia nods and manages a small smile.

'Dale. Your help is so very much appreciated. Please, come with me to the police so we can tell them what you just told me, and they can find Melvin and my sister. Please! Before it's too late.'

Dale shakes his head furiously.

'You don't understand. They still have my boys, and they will hurt them if anyone knows I helped you. I can't do that to them. They know I'm here too. You can do what you want with this information, but never mention me or my boys.'

Lydia is sympathetic, and nods her head solemnly in response. Dale is obviously terrified of Melvin and his family.

'But, how can we ever stop these people, if you

don't lead us to them? There are some good people, experts with this kind of thing, who might be able to get you back with your sons, Dale.'

But Dale is staring out the window, and his eyes are glazed again. He hugs himself, and rocks back and forth. Lydia looks at the door; she knows she needs to speak to the police immediately with this information, but without her phone, she's stuck. She tells Dale she needs to go, but will be back later, and they will come up with a plan. She reaches down to pick up Molly's lead and the little dog looks very happy to be leaving. Dale jumps up from the bed, and walks to the door, then turns, and stands in front of it, blocking the way. Lydia is terrified. He won't let her leave. Molly barks. Dale's eyes open widely, he stares straight ahead at the wall behind Lydia, then crashes to the ground, and starts to shake uncontrollably, his entire body is in convulsions. Lydia thinks quickly, and puts a pillow behind his head, before opening the door and running downstairs to get help.

36

Kate has been awake all night, and so has Christine.
When Kate was on the landing, about to try to escape,
Christine had been lying in the dark next to Melvin,
thinking about how bad the bruising would be on her
face after what had happened earlier. He had obviously
drank quite a lot after he hit her, and he stank of
alcohol. His sleep was light and fitful; sometimes he
muttered a little bit, but Christine couldn't make out
what he was saying. He often drank after an outburst
like that, and it could go either way; the alcohol could
calm him down, or it could reignite his aggressive
behaviour, so that he started to hit or humiliate her
again. Christine had lain there, pretending to be asleep,
when he seemed to stir for some reason. Then, Melvin
had gone to the bathroom, but after a few minutes she
heard him unlocking the door to Kate's room, and she
had sat up in the bed, listening. She had never heard
him rape somebody before. She knew that he was
doing it to Kate most nights after she had come here,
and only stopped when she got pregnant. But, tonight
had nothing to do with trying to get someone pregnant,
and nothing to do with a prophecy. Christine
remembered the sexual attacks she had suffered as a
girl at the ranch. It started when she was about thirteen,
and she had been told they were tests of faith and
strength, or punishments for not being a good enough
person. And when Melanie came here last year and
Melvin raped her, he told Christine it was to get her
pregnant in case she was 'the one'. Tonight, Christine
had waited for it to end, for Melvin to leave Kate's
room and return to bed, and as every minute went by,
she realised that she felt nothing for him anymore,

except hate. Something had broken in her. If it wasn't for the prophecy and the baby that Kate was carrying, Christine decided she would want to leave. The thought was entirely shocking to her, and she wondered if she would feel the same way in the morning, or in a few days when she had forgotten about the attack.

Morning came, and Kate waited for Christine to come and take her to the bathroom. She wasn't in pain and she hadn't resisted Melvin, but she couldn't wait to wash his stink from her. She had to lie here all night, for hours, covered in it; his sweat, the smell of alcohol, the semen caked on her thighs. It made her gag worse than she ever had, and she wondered if pregnancy had made her more sensitive to it. He had come in here and asked if she was awake. Terrified that he knew she had opened the door, Kate sat up in the bed and tried to ease his mind. When he saw her hands were untied she quickly explained what had happened and waited as he pieced the story together. He remembered coming home without a key and having to wait for Christine to let him in, and he remembered hitting her for being so lazy and stupid. Yes, he remembered Kate had been tired, and could see that her hands being untied was Christine's fault, not Kate's. He would beat her again tomorrow, he thought to himself. He would tell her that he will kill her the next time she did something like that, and threaten with locking her in the basement for a couple of nights. He had laughed as he tied Kate's hands together again, as he pulled off her leggings and forced himself inside of her. He had tried to kiss her, which he had done from time to time in the first few months, and Kate had found herself frozen and rigid, like she was dead. She couldn't forgive herself for what was happening in front of her unborn child, and she worried that this sickness would affect the baby, somehow. With every thrust, grunt, and sensation that was forced on her, she imagined she was back on the landing, and instead of running back into bed, to this; instead of allowing this soul-destroying thing to be done to her again, she imagined she had run out the front door, climbed the wall, run through the woods, across the fields, and into the free world.

This morning, Christine comes into the room with a fresh purple bruise on her cheekbone. Her eyes are bloodshot from the sleepless night, and Kate knows that she knows. She can also sense that the energy has shifted, and Kate is no longer the safe, pregnant mother of what Melvin thinks is the messiah. They are both victims of his violent, evil side. They both know that Christine was beaten and Kate was raped last night. Just yesterday afternoon they had sat on this very bed eating crisps and chatting, and now everything was heavy, slow, and unbearable. Without knowing it, the two women are thinking the same thing: that Melvin has taken a turn, and things might get even worse for everyone, very soon.

37

McCarthy and Davies arrive at the Royal Free Hospital early; they want to see Dale Adams as soon as they can. Brian and Lydia Stone had called the day before with information about Dale, and that he said he knew the man who took Kate. But, Dale was kept in for observation overnight after suffering a severe epileptic fit. They had to sit tight.

They enter the ward now, McCarthy shows his badge to one of the nurses on duty, and tells her that they need to speak to Dale Adams immediately, in conjunction with a missing person case. The nurse says that Dale is stable enough, and leads them to his bed. She stands next to Davies as the men introduce themselves, and then McCarthy asks her for some privacy.

'I'll be right here, Mr Adams, if you need anything. Alright?'

She seems concerned about Dale, and waits for him to respond, before moving away from the bed.

'Th-thanks Sophie.' Dale responds.

Dale's face is drooped to one side, and McCarthy wonders if he's had a stroke. As soon as Dale starts to speak it's obvious that he is also suffering mentally. He seems confused and disorientated. McCarthy excuses himself for a moment, and quietly asks Davies to stall things by getting them all some tea. He needs to speak to the nurse.

Nurse Sophie Thurston is happy to speak to McCarthy, and suggests they sit on some chairs in the corridor, while Davies searches for a vending machine downstairs. She seems like a warm, genuine person, and tells McCarthy she believes Dale is virtually homeless, and gets a bed-sit in a sort of charity-run halfway house from time to time.

'He's got lots of disabilities, and has problems with his speech and hearing. He spent the night crying last night, and I was on duty, so I actually ended up just listening to him and trying to calm him down.'

'Has he been diagnosed with anything that I should know about?'

'No, detective. He's been in this hospital before, a few times actually, and he's an epileptic. But other than that... I just think he's a pretty damaged guy. So, go easy on him?'

'Did he mention anything to you about someone called Kate Stone; a missing girl?'

'No. Nothing like that. He just spoke about his dead wife, and his sons in America.'

McCarthy nods and stands up, thanks the nurse for her help, then walks back to the ward. Dale seems to be more coherent now with a cup of tea in his hand, and Davies is chatting to him about the recession, and how difficult it is to find work in London. Davies is good at putting people at ease, and as annoying as he can be, some people respond much better to him than they do to McCarthy. McCarthy asks him if he knows where Kate Stone is, or if he has ever met her, and Dale repeats what he told Lydia. He tells them that Barbara Stone, the woman he knows as Margaret Pernot, and her sister Cassie escaped a cult in the US, the same group that Dale and his family were involved in, and he ended up escaping with them. He hadn't planned on leaving, and was actually in charge of making sure Barbara and her sister were safe and secure when they ran. They essentially tricked him. Then, knowing that he would be killed if he returned to camp without them, he ran too. The three of them left the country, paying for false passports and ID with money the girls had stolen.

'It was a prophecy that the whole thing was built on you see, that Melvin Todd who was the son of the founder of the church, and Margaret, who you know as Barbara Stone, would have a child together. She got away before that could happen, but the group got bigger and stronger, and they did not give up on having that prophecy fulfilled.'

McCarthy has written a few things down and asks Dale if he would be able to do an official interview with the police later on today. He can see by Dale's face that he's not happy about that. He looks scared.

'Mr Adams, we need your help. I promise that your identity will be safe in all this.'

Dale nods reluctantly and tells McCarthy that he will make his own way to the station when they let him out. Davies and McCarthy glance at one another. It feels wrong, asking a man in his condition to do that, and they offer to send a car for him, instead.

'You just tell the nice nurse over there to make the call, and I'll give her the correct number for me. Alright? There can be a car here to take you to us at the station in Hendon in about half an hour.'

Dale seems relieved about the new plan, and tells them he'll see them later.

'Get some rest today, Mr Adams. Hopefully we will see you later on then.'

McCarthy and Davies have a quick word with Nurse Thurston, and she agrees to call when Dale is okay to be released; probably this afternoon.

They go back to the station, and McCarthy wracks his brains about what to do next; he needs to use his US contacts, and calls Jared Cooper. He fills him in about the progress in the Stone case, and says he needs his help.

Lydia had told Jared everything about Dale and the cult already, as well as what the police had said the evening before, and he guessed that they would be moving quickly this morning. He's already found a cult expert in the States that he's worked with before called Lana Nowicki, and he offers to speak to her on the phone and run any names past her. McCarthy tells him about Melvin Todd and asks him to see if Lana knows anything about him. When they say their goodbyes, Jared immediately calls Lana. It's 6AM in New York, but she answers the phone after two rings. She's been waiting for this call.

Lydia, Brian, and Ida are sitting in the Stone's living room, and a photograph of Melanie Latter is open on a laptop screen in front of them. Jared had shown it to Lydia in private, and now she needs Ida to confirm this is the girl from her visions before they do anything else. She's clutching her face with one hand, and the other hand is touching the screen. Tears fill her eyes as she traces the outline of Melanie's smile with her fingertips. Brian looks concerned at how upset she is; over the past months, Lydia had told him all about Ida, her house, her cat, how sweet she was, but he had remained quite cynical about the whole thing, and part of him assumed she was deluded or a con artist. But, today he had met a true lady. Ida was no con artist. Brian trusted his gut, and he trusted her. She was so fragile, open, and softly spoken. Brian felt what Lydia had felt when she first went to Ida's house; like she was the grandma he never had; that sort of charismatic gentleness and warmth she exuded made you just want to hug her.

'That's her. That's the girl from my visions.' Ida suddenly whispers. She apologises for crying, and tells them that she can't seem to stop the tears these days. Lydia reassuringly puts a hand on Ida's arm, and tries to offer some comfort.

'It's okay to be sad, Ida. Maybe now that you've seen her, and know her name is Melanie... maybe now the visions will stop.'

Ida is thinking the same thing. In fact, she knows in her heart that the visions will stop, and even now, she can feel the dark veil lifting a little. But, she's got a new heaviness in her mind, the Latter family. Will they want to know what Ida saw, and how she thinks Melanie died?

'I can't tell them.' Ida blurts out, shaking her head from side to side.

'I can't tell her family what I saw in those visions and dreams. It's too horrific. Nobody should have to hear that about their child.'

Then, remembering that the Stones have also lost someone, and are fearing the worst, she apologises. She looks from Lydia to Brian, and can see the worry and pain in their eyes.

'I haven't seen Kate in the same way. You both know that.'

They nod, and tell Ida that it's okay, and she can't worry about them. Brian changes the subject, and asks Lydia if she can find any photographs of Melanie's family. She's already found all of them on Facebook, and printed out the details about where Melanie went missing and any clues they had about what had happened to her. There were seven or eight online articles containing interviews with a few of her friends that were there that night, and her parents of course. She shows Brian the photos of Melanie's parents on the screen, and he looks closely, feeling like he recognises them, somehow. Lydia has already told her dad about Melvin Todd and all of the things that Dale had told her the day before, and she fills Ida in now, too. It's all in line with the visions that Ida had about the cult, and her mother being part of it, then running away to start a new life with a new name in the UK.

'Ida, it's all starting to make sense. Like a crazy amount of sense! You knew this. Your gift helped us to uncover all of this!'

Lydia is actually smiling through her tears. She excuses herself and goes upstairs to make a quick call to Jared. He doesn't pick up, so she leaves a voice message to say that Melanie is the one from Ida's visions. She checks her watch as she descends the stairs, and is shocked to see it's only midday. It's frustrating not to know what is going on with Dale and the police. They might have found out where Melvin is by now, but no-one has told her. There has to be something she can do in the mean time to move this along. Her thoughts flash to her mother in the psychiatric ward, and a familiar, heavy anger and frustration rises in her chest. What was going to make her break and start telling them the truth? Now, they could go to her and say they knew about Melvin, Dale, and all about her and her sister changing their names. Lydia feels like screaming, like ripping something apart. Her mother is a liar. Lydia was raised by a liar, and her sister isn't here now because of those lies. She wonders how she will even have the strength to face her mum again. If Barbara continues to hide the truth, Lydia wants nothing to do with her. She doesn't care if she dies. She almost deserves to, Lydia thinks. If she had told the police about the cult and Melvin months ago, then Kate might have been found by now. How could she be so stupid and selfish? How could she let fear of her past, cloud the present?

Lydia re-joins Ida and her father and tells them that they have to speak to her mum. Brian gets up and puts his arm around her.

'I'm not sure that will help, darling. We don't want to push her any more than she's already been pushed, you know? She's really not well.'

Lydia moves away from him, and walks to the sofa. Ida shifts uncomfortably in her seat.

'Dad, she might know where Kate is. Don't you get

that? She knows this Melvin guy, this psychopath, and she might even know where he is right now!'

Brian crosses one hand over his stomach, and leans on it with the elbow of his other arm, stroking his beard. He thinks, his eyes on the floor, then looks up at Ida, who smiles back kindly. Then his eyes meet Lydia's. In that moment, he is so proud of her. She has been through so much trauma and pain recently; losing her sister, her mother trying to kill herself, and lying to them, and he hasn't been much of a father either.

'Lyds. I'm so sorry. You're right. We have to ask. Let's go now.'

Lydia breathes a sigh of relief, and gets up to leave, telling Ida that they can drop her home on the way.

39

McCarthy finishes a meeting with his team at Hendon station and returns to his office, sits at the desk, and opens an email from Lydia Stone. It's only a short paragraph. It says she's been working with a psychic who believes her sister is alive and is the same man that took Melanie Latter last year from Banbury in Oxfordshire. Lydia's final sentence reads:

'Melvin Todd, the man that Dale Adams believes took Kate and knows my mother, may have taken Melanie too. Please speak to her family and find out if there is a connection? Please, Detective McCarthy.'

McCarthy leans back in his chair. He has never worked on a case like this. It just got stranger and stranger. How was it that Lydia Stone found out about Melanie? Was it really via a psychic? And how strange a coincidence that Jared Cooper had mentioned it so recently. He remembers the CCTV footage of the man in the mask that they retrieved from Haven from the night that Kate went missing. Whoever was behind that mask probably knew where Kate was, and whether she was alive or dead. He also knew what he was doing, and as far as McCarthy was concerned, it was highly unlikely that he acted alone. This Dale Adams seemed to appear out of nowhere. Lydia had said that she saw him outside the Stone's home a couple of months after Kate went missing, and it did seem like he knew Barbara, but what if he was involved in some other way, or without realising it, he had led Melvin Todd to the Stones. They would have to wait until they interviewed him later today before they could put anything into action. Suddenly, there's a knock on the open door and Jared asks if he can have a word. He's been speaking to the contact of his in New York, Lana Nowicki, who thinks she can help. Lana is a cult expert and knows who Melvin Todd is. When he hears this, McCarthy closes the door, and invites Jared to have a seat. Jared nods and accepts but continues to talk. Lana looked into the cult that was run by Joseph Todd known as The Church of the Family of the Prophecy, or 'CFP', in the late nineties, after the remains of twenty-three females, mostly children, were found in a quarry near where one branch of the group used to live. She had travelled to the area and interviewed a few ex members of the group, trying to pinpoint who was responsible for the deaths and who the children and women were. The case was huge, according to Lana, but they ran out of funding after a year or so, and they were no closer to finding out the truth. The cult lived off-grid, and many of them had changed their names and moved around a lot. They were essentially living like travellers, didn't register births or deaths, didn't have any attachment to society outside of the church, and they were extremely secretive. Melvin Todd and a few other core members of the group went missing over ten years ago, and Lana thinks they obtained false identities and moved overseas.

'Do you think Melvin could be here, in the UK?' McCarthy asks Jared.

'It's entirely possible. This group, church, cult, whatever you want to call it, was very large and had 'families' all over the states. These people don't just disappear overnight, you know? Lana thinks they just moved and became more secretive. They don't have any sort of online presence and they don't recruit in obvious ways.'

McCarthy puts his hand up to stop Jared from

speaking.

'Does she have a photograph of this guy? Melvin?'

Jared nods. Lana has emailed Jared with a few photographs of the Todd family. He pulls his laptop from his bag and when he opens it, they stare into the face of Melvin Todd. It's dated 1999, and looks like it was taken in some kind of photo booth at a fair. He's eyes are large and sunken, his cheekbones protruding. He reminds McCarthy of Charles Manson, with the same delirious twinkle in his eye.

'This was an image that a few ex-members actually had on their fridges, or whatever. They worshipped the Todd family like they were directly connected to God himself.'

The next few photos are of Joseph Todd, Melvin's father, and then a group shot of what Lana believes are the elders in the church, including both of the Todd men. McCarthy stares at the screen closely, as Jared flicks between images. His mind furiously pieces together the bits of this strange jigsaw puzzle. A missing girl who may have been kidnapped by a cult leader because of a prophecy involving the girl's mother. Could it really be possible? The human race never ceased to amaze McCarthy. Some people are deluded and dangerous. He nods at Jared, and thanks him for the great work; he will make a plan and get back to him. McCarthy asks him to speak to Melanie Latter's family in the meantime, on the off-chance that they are in any way connected to the Stones. They need to know if Melanie and Kate are connected in any way at all. Jared is happy to help, and has actually briefly spoken with the Latters before.

'I'll let you know as soon as I speak to them.'

He leaves the office, and sends a quick text to Lydia:

'Spoke to McCarthy. They are taking this seriously. Call me when you can x'

There is every chance that photographs of Melvin Todd could be in circulation very soon if McCarthy and the team have reason to believe he may know where Kate Stone is. Then, Jared has a thought: they need Barbara Stone to see a photograph of Melvin. That could be a way to break her; show her the guy who might have her daughter. Surely, it's worth a shot? Then she might talk? He walks back to McCarthy's office, and suggests that the photograph could be used with the Stone family to see if they recognise him or to trigger Barbara to talk. McCarthy is already on it.

'Absolutely Jared. Thanks again'

A slightly embarrassed Jared walks down the hall. He is desperate to tell Lydia what's going on, but he can't be seen to share evidence with anyone. He just has to trust that McCarthy knows what he's doing.

40

Barbara is finding it difficult to keep any food down. It feels like she has been in this hospital for an eternity and she's not getting any better. She longs to be at home, in her own bed with her family around her. But that seems like a distant memory; almost like it never even happened and she never really had a family. She also has an intense longing to get out of here, and out of this life. The medication they put her on makes her feel heavy and numb; like they've filled her veins with a slow-moving, thick liquid, instead of blood, and her brain doesn't work properly any more. She can feel a certain amount of emotion, but just before it's fully realised, it drifts away, and is replaced by numbness and confusion again. She thinks about Kate, and can feel herself becoming sad, but she can't quite feel the sadness. Everything is dulled down, and she is starting to feel like a robot. The nurses just tell her to rest, and the doctors stare at her like she is some sort of broken-down vehicle. She feels powerless, useless, lost.

Lydia is shaking as she walks down the corridor towards her mother's room. Her dad tries to put his arm around her in support, but she pushes him away. This is hard for her; she's terrified about what her mum might tell them, but also scared that she might still deny everything. Right now, Lydia doesn't want to have anything to do with her, unless she starts telling the truth. They stop outside the room, and the nurse tells them that she has had a few bad nights and the doctors don't think the new medications are working very well. Brian asks the nurse to give them a moment alone and agrees to speak to her afterwards. He walks into the room and immediately reaches out to touch his wife's face. When she opens her eyes and sees him, he explains that Lydia has come to see her, too. Barbara smiles and opens her arms to her daughter. Lydia walks to her and leans down for a hug, but pulls away quickly. Immediately, Barbara can see something is wrong, and pushes herself up in bed so she can see them both properly.

'What's happened? Why are you both looking like that?'

She looks from her daughter to her husband, asking again what's happened, and she tries to hold it together for as long as she can. She must find out what's going on. Then, Lydia clears her throat, and looks her mother in the eye.

'Mum, who is Melvin Todd?'

Barbara opens her dry mouth in an audible gasp. She lets her head fall back on to the pillows, and her eyes close in horror. She doesn't have the strength or foresight to hide her reaction. His name makes her heart sink, and her skin feel cold. It feels like death just thinking about him. Brian and Lydia glance at one another, then sit on either side of Barbara. Brian reaches out and puts his hand on his wife's hand. Seeing her in so much pain suddenly becomes unbearable to him.

'My darling, it's okay. You can tell us now, alright?'

As he gets the words out, Brian's voice breaks into a sob, and he has to put a hand to his mouth to stop. Lydia has never seen him like this, and is momentarily distracted. She leans across, and puts a reassuring hand on his shoulder and tells him it's okay.

'Mum, the police know about Melvin Todd and the cult. The secret's out, Mum. There's another man called Dale Adams... I assume you know who we mean? Well, he's talking now, too. You're the only one who is keeping this secret.'

Barbara wasn't expecting this. All of a sudden, the fear and panic at the mention of Melvin's name is replaced with something else; a fire, and movement of some kind that stirs in her chest. If they know already, then maybe she has no choice but to talk, she thinks. Maybe her worst fear; the thing she thought must be impossible; that they would come after her after all these years and hurt her family, maybe it had happened. And Dale Adams must have finally found out where she lived. She knew they couldn't trust him to keep quiet. He hadn't even changed his name. He could have been the one to lead them to Kate! Brian sees the panic on his wife's face.

'Please, Barbara. Please help us, and the police to find Kate. Tell us what happened. You don't need to hide anymore.'

As he looks at her, Brian can feel the love he has for his wife and family flooding into the room. As they are looking into one another's tear-filled eyes, he wants more than anything for her to be okay. He is going to fight for this family, but he needs her help. Lydia joins in:

'Mum, we still love you. We still love you, but we need you now, Mum.'

Barbara reaches out to hold Lydia's hand, and nods to her daughter in response.

'I'm so sorry. I'm so sorry I did this to you.'

Barbara starts to cry uncontrollably. The nurse comes over to see what's the matter, and suggests she might need some rest.

'No! This is my chance to make it right. Please, I need them here.'

The nurse reluctantly leaves them to it, but watches

from the doorway. Barbara blows her nose, and passes the box of tissues to Brian and Lydia. She takes a deep breath, and starts to tell them about her life at the ranch. Lydia and Brian try to be strong, but from the very beginning it's heart-breaking, and they both have to fight to keep the tears back. Barbara's voice is weak, and they need to sit very close to hear what she's saying. She tells them that when she was fifteen, and her sister, Jane was twelve, the family moved from Minneapolis, Minnesota, to San Diego, California. They wanted more sunshine, and thought they would be happier there. But, a few months after they moved, the family started to struggle; her father got sick, was diagnosed with multiple sclerosis, couldn't work, and her mother didn't make much money working in a local convenience store. The girls also struggled to fit in at school. California wasn't turning out to be the dream they had all imagined. One day, Barbara's mother came home and was excited about something. She had met a woman at the store who lived in a gated community that was a kind of private church called The Church of the Family of the Prophecy, or CFP for short. There were about twenty families in the community, they home-schooled their kids, and shared all of their money. She invited Barbara's mother to visit them, and after meeting with a few of the people that ran the community, they wanted the family to consider joining them. Barbara doesn't really remember much about the members of the community in California, but she remembers that when she and her sister went to their first meeting at the compound, one of the older men in the group took a special interest in her and wanted to take a photograph of her. She thought that was weird. He said that people could tell a lot by a photograph and that he had a feeling that if he showed it to the church leaders, he was pretty sure they would be invited to join. Barbara didn't know it at the time, but the church was built on the prophecy of one man; Joseph Todd. The prophecy said that his son, Melvin, would father the next messiah and he would save the world and everyone in it from war, disease, and suffering. Joseph claimed to have had a series of visions, dreams, and actual conversations with God describing the mother of this baby. She would be young, a virgin of course, and have a very specific physical appearance: very long, dark, straight hair that was parted in the middle, large dark eyes, a slender figure, and an olive complexion. Joseph Todd had been speaking of this girl for over ten years and there were many sketches and paintings in circulation depicting her. When the elders from the California wing of the CFP laid eyes on Barbara, they believed she could be 'The One'. The photograph was posted to church HQ in Texas immediately and although they were not aware of it at that time, Joseph Todd told them to do anything they could to get the family to Texas immediately. He had to meet this girl. At that point, Barbara's parents were actually pretty desperate. They didn't have health insurance and her father's condition was deteriorating quickly. Within three weeks of meeting the church, they were given the keys to a beautiful house near the compound in San Diego, thousands of dollars to pay off their debts and buy new clothes, and Barbara's mother even had some much-needed dental work done. She stopped working at the convenience store, and started working at the compound, instead.

'No-one ever thought to ask where the money came from. We thought that we were just in the right place at the right time, and this was maybe the reason that we came to California in the first place. My mother was superstitious, and probably very gullible too. She always saw the best in people, and was blind to the fact that bad things happened.'

Lydia and Brian are transfixed by the story. The nurse comes into the room with some tea and sandwiches, and Barbara continues to talk, taking sips of sugary tea from time to time. She tells them about the decision to move to Texas. It seemed to happen pretty much overnight. They were told they would have to move out of the house they were in after a few weeks, and that they were one of the lucky families who would be offered the opportunity to live on the Texas ranch. The other compound members seemed genuinely surprised and envious that this new family were invited to live in the main ranch; the one where Joseph Todd, their leader, resided. Of course, everyone in the Californian branch knew that Barbara was potentially part of the prophecy, and their excitement and encouragement made the move seem like the obvious answer. They had only been in California for five months when they packed their few belongings up and got on a plane to Dallas. They had two men travelled with them, sorting out everything from check-in, to snacks and rental cars. Even then, Barbara recognised that they were getting special treatment and she couldn't help but feel excited about what the future would hold.

The ranch itself was in the middle of nowhere, and Barbara remembers falling asleep in the van on the four-hour journey from the airport to their new life. When they arrived at the ranch, the vastness of the CFP community hit them. There seemed to be hundreds of people there, and much more security too. When they got out of the van, they were greeted by about twenty men who removed their hats and shook hands with them. They were shown to a wooden cabin with three bedrooms, a large open-plan living space, a patio, garden swing, and hammock. The fridge in the kitchen was filled with food and in the girls' bedroom was a large dresser with flowers and chocolates on it. Barbara remembers Jane crying when she realised that there was a special gift for Barbara, but nothing for her. It was a silver dragonfly necklace. Joseph Todd and his son Melvin introduced themselves properly that evening, and Melvin told Barbara that the gift was from him.

'I had no idea what was happening. I suppose I thought they liked me, thought I was beautiful. I don't know. I just wanted to sleep, wake up the next day, and spend time with my family.'

Barbara describes the next few weeks and months; the realisation that all of the other families on the ranch lived in camps or trailers. Some were dirty and looked ill. There also seemed to be a high number of mentally unwell people at the ranch, and although they all prayed together every day in the large barn-like church, there seemed to be a great amount of unrest amongst families. Barbara saw a knife fight a couple of weeks after they arrived, and was pretty sure that one of the men involved died afterwards. She was pulled away by her mother but she heard one of the men cry out in agony. She never saw him after that, and no-one ever spoke about him again.

'It was strange. The people were very weird, but I was being treated so well, and we just went along with it.'

But things changed for Barbara. One day, she was told that she was going to marry Melvin Todd. Nobody asked her, and she had barely had a conversation with the man. Plus, he was in his thirties, and only a few years younger than her own parents. Melvin told her about the prophecy, and the fact that they were going to have a baby together. It was all too much for Barbara. She was terrified. She begged her parents to leave, but they were too entrenched in life at the ranch. Plus, her father's health meant that he was mostly bedridden. Then two months after they moved there, he died suddenly. The circumstances surrounding his death were suspicious; it happened while they were all at church listening to Joseph Todd preaching. A few of the men who usually sat up front were not at the service that day and Barbara thought it strange. She immediately thought they had something to do with his death, and she and her mother were ordered not to tell anyone about it outside of the ranch. Her mother was heart-broken after that, and seemed to just disappear from that day on. Then, Barbara was raped by two teenage boys one night a few days after that, and it changed everything. She ran home to tell her mother, and her mother told her not to tell anyone, because they would no longer see her as part of the prophecy. Nothing would protect them if they didn't believe she was special. But, Barbara was suffering with shock and ended up telling a couple of the women she was friendly with. Melvin and Joseph found out and went crazy. The boys who raped her were beaten publicly and never seen again. Joseph believed that the prophecy was ruined, and now Barbara couldn't be the mother of the messiah or marry Melvin. They moved her to a dorm house with about twenty other girls and she was separated from her sister and mother.

'I'm not sure how much to tell you both. Basically, things got really bad, and I was forced to become part of lots of these... rituals. I was beaten and raped and I think I would have died if it wasn't for Joseph changing his mind. Other girls died though, and I witnessed that.'

Barbara closes her eyes for a moment as the memory of the little girl she was forced to push from the cliff comes into her mind. Lydia and Brian have been silent for the past fifteen minutes. They cannot believe what they're hearing. How could she have gone through all of this and never told anyone? They continue to listen as Barbara explains how Joseph claimed to have had another vision where the mother of the messiah was tested and proved herself to be strong and good. He called the entire community together and announced that Barbara was still 'The One', and although she had been stained with the filth of sin and violence, her heart was so full of light, that it didn't matter. Melvin went along with it too, and after just a few weeks of living in the dorm with the other girls who were being horrifically victimised and used, Barbara was allowed to go back to the house. But her mother and sister were instructed to stay in their dorms. From then on, she only saw them occasionally, and each time that she did, she could see them deteriorate more and more. Her mother was slowly becoming a zombie, and looked like she was drugged or drunk. Barbara begged Melvin and Joseph to let her mother and sister come home, but Joseph told her that God didn't want them to be together. She had to stay 'pure', and concentrate on her future role as wife and mother. At this point the community saw Melvin and

Barbara as a married couple. They had a small ceremony at the house conducted by Joseph Todd, and Melvin moved in. After a few months, Barbara's mother died. The community said that she had drank too much and fallen in the quarry, hitting her head. But Barbara didn't believe it. She knew that they wanted to get rid of her.

'I thought that Jane would be next, so I begged and begged that she be allowed to come and live with us. I convinced Melvin and his father that the reason I hadn't fallen pregnant yet was because I was sick with worry about her. So, he agreed and Jane and I were reunited. That's when we hatched our plan, and got Dale Adams to help us escape, we stole some money from the church, and flew to England.'

Lydia can see that her mother is exhausted. Telling them all of this must have used the little bit of energy she had. She tells her to eat some of the cheese sandwich in front of her, and asks her dad if they should call McCarthy.

41

Kate has spent the day pretending to be ill. Every time she's alone, she does everything she can to make her face as hot and red as possible. Christine confirms that she has a temperature, and as the day goes by, she and Melvin grow increasingly worried. Kate tells them she needs to walk around, needs air, can't breathe. She does a great job at making them believe she really is suffering, and she watches as Melvin becomes more and more worried about the baby. He flicks through pregnancy books looking for answers, and agrees to untie Kate's hands completely when she asks him to, without a second thought. She knows it's a long shot to think they might leave her untied all night again, but she has to try.

Evening comes, and the moon appears, full this time. Kate pretends to be sound asleep, as she had before, and can't believe it when she first hears Melvin, then Christine, pop their heads round the door to check on her, then go to bed. She thought that surely one of them would come back in to check she was secured to the bed, but thirty or forty minutes pass, then an hour, and soon Kate realises she has another chance to get out of here. Once she has opened the lock again with the piece of metal from the lampshade, she steps out on to the landing and makes her way for the stairs. She places a foot on the first step, and quietly and skilfully moves to the second, third, fourth. She uses the bannister to take as much weight off her feet as possible, and it seems to work; she has descended almost silently. When she reaches the bottom of the, she stops suddenly, convinced that she's heard something. She remembers the bedroom door that she's left open.

If either Melvin or Christine even get up to go to the bathroom, they will know what she's done. Adrenaline courses its way through Kate's body. It's cold down here, and she only has bed socks, leggings, and a couple of jumpers to keep her warm. It's not enough. She concentrates on her breathing, and that keeps her relatively calm. She thinks to herself that she has nothing to lose at this stage, and steps on to the carpeted hallway. Kate has only been downstairs once when they moved her up from the basement, but she recognises it. The front door is down the hall to Kate's left, and through the door in front of her is the living room. It's right under her bedroom. To the right is what looks like a laundry or storage room, and then another door that leads to the kitchen and another to a reception room. Kate takes a few steps towards the front door. She can smell the cold, fresh, country air. Just a few feet away is freedom, and the outside world. She longs for it so much, and wants to open the door and run all the way to London, back to her family. But, she stays calm and collected, and knows that if she puts a foot wrong, everything could come crashing down. Next to her, about halfway down the hallway is a small table with an old-fashioned green telephone on it. Kate moves closer. If she could make a call to the police, everything would change. They might be able to trace the call, and find her here. She peers down at the phone and can see that there is some sort of homemade lock around it, like a bicycle lock wrapped around the receiver and under the base of the phone, making it impossible to use. At first, Kate assumes that Melvin probably has the key on the chain around his neck, but then she starts to look around the hall for other places it could be. She peers into a plant pot to find it's empty, and then spots a small wooden book shelf at head height, with what looks like an ashtray on top of it. Kate take a closer look. There's something inside. Suddenly, there's a noise from upstairs and she hears footsteps making their way across the ceiling. Kate takes a sharp intake of breath; he's going to kill her. Before she can think what to do next, she looks down and sees a small silver key sitting in the ashtray. It looks like the right size for the phone lock. But, it's too late to do anything about it now. Footsteps descend the stairs.

Christine had decided not to wake Melvin when she saw that Kate's door was open. He would kill her if Kate had escaped and blame Christine for not tying her up properly. Kate has dropped to the floor, and pretended that she fainted. Christine shakes her, and in a hushed voice tries to wake her.

'Get up, for the love of God, or he will kill us both! Do you hear me?'

Kate can't believe her plan is working. Christine seems to genuinely think she's ill, and just fainted as she wandered around the house. She stirs at Christine's touch, and mumbles something about not feeling well, and wanting her mother. Christine helps her to her feet, asking if the baby is okay, and Kate tells her that she didn't fall but had to lay down as she was so tired and the baby is fine. Somehow the pair make it to Kate's room without waking Melvin, and Kate climbs into bed, immediately closing her eyes and pretending to be asleep. But Christine switches the lamp on, ties Kate's hands to the long chain, and sits on the bed, shaking her again, gently this time.

'What happened tonight? How did you get out of this room?'

Kate looks at her sleepily and smiles.

'I wanted my mum, and the door was open. You must have forgotten to lock it. I just wanted to get some water and se-see Mum.'

Christine tries to remember if she locked the door. If she had forgotten and that was how Kate got downstairs, Melvin would probably kill her. She needs to fix this.

'Kate, we can't tell him.'

Kate nods sleepily.

'If he finds out, we're both in serious trouble. Do NOT tell him. Understand?'

Kate opens her eyes, and reaches out for her hand. Christine almost flinches at the sensation. She's not used to anyone touching her.

'I promise, Christine. It was a mistake. No way am I going to say anything. I don't either of us to get into trouble.'

Satisfied, Christine switches the light out, and leaves the room. She struggles to lock the door behind her, and Kate winces, scared that she'll realise what Kate did after all. But eventually, it locks somehow.

Kate lies awake staring at the ceiling. Tonight has brought her one step closer to escaping; all she needs to do now, is find a window of opportunity when she's untied, even in the daytime, and she can go downstairs, unlock the phone with the key, and make that call.

42

Dale Adams sits in the interview room at Hendon police station. He's obviously not a very well man and rocks back and forth continuously. His arms are unbelievably thin; in fact, his whole body looks like it's being eaten away from the inside out, and there are sores and cuts on his hands and face. The effects of sleeping rough for years are devastating, and his skin is damaged from the cold, malnourishment, and lack of sleep. McCarthy shows Dale a photograph of Kate Stone and asks if he knows her. Dale tells him that he knows that she is missing and as he has already told them, he knows her mother, Margaret. McCarthy shows him a photograph of Barbara Stone and Dale tells them that's the woman he knows as Margaret. He goes on to explain that he left the CFP church over twenty years ago, and fled to England with Margaret and her sister, Cassie. The girls had special privileges in the church and he was assigned as a temporary bodyguard to them at one stage. His wife had died, and he was seriously contemplating leaving the church anyway, because his life had been threatened by a couple of the elders, but he had two sons at a different branch in a different State and had no way of getting them out safely. When Margaret and Cassie were only sixteen and thirteen, they had stolen around ten thousand dollars from a safe in the compound, and convinced Dale to leave with them and fly to Europe. Dale had a passport from before they entered the church that he could get renewed, and the girls had managed to keep theirs, too. But, they needed an adult to travel with them as they were both under eighteen. He had said no at first, but when they ran one night and Dale couldn't stop them, he decided to join them in their plan, after all; fearing that if he returned without them he would undoubtedly be killed. Dale goes on to explain what happened after they arrived in England. The girls had simply left him at the airport with a few hundred pounds, and told him to be careful. He had been entirely lost on the streets of London, and ended up becoming a drug addict. He had also been homeless for the past four or five years, apart from the occasional stay in a hostel or state-funded rehabilitation unit, like the one he was staying in at the moment.

'And how did you come to see Mrs Stone, and recognise her?' McCarthy asks.

'I only knew her daughter was missing when I saw the family photograph in one of the free newspapers. It said they lived in Hampstead, and that was only around the corner. It was purely by chance I saw her one day when I was walking down the street there, and I couldn't believe it. I called out to her, but she ignored me; didn't want to know. I walked up the road and saw her car outside a big fancy house, but when I asked her daughter, Lydia if she lived there, she didn't know anything about it or who Margaret was. I knew they were going to change their names and all that, but I didn't think she would ignore me.'

The interview goes on for over three hours, and eventually they see that Dale is exhausted, and decide to let him go.

'Your help has been incredible Mr Adams. You are doing a really good thing here, and we won't forget it, okay? I'm so sorry for what happened to you.'

'If you find them, those bastards that killed my wife and have my sons, my two boys, help me to get them back, will you?'

McCarthy nods solemnly. He knows he can't promise this man anything. His sons could be anywhere.

'We will let you know if we find anything, Mr Adams. You have my word. You can reach me any time on the same number you called today. Please, stay in touch.'

Before Dale leaves, McCarthy asks one of the office assistants to give him some meal vouchers for the cafe down the road, and a basic mobile phone with twenty pounds credit on it. That way, they have more of a chance of reaching him if and when they need to. Dale looks thrilled at the prospect of having a new phone, and thanks them profusely. McCarthy feels a pang of guilt, and wishes he could do more, but at least they can maybe get some answers about his sons.

McCarthy walks down the hall to his office, and picks up the phone. He needs to get an update from Lana in New York.

43

In Florida, Jane answers the phone on the second ring. It's Brian on the other end. Barbara has already texted her to say that that Brian, Lydia, and the police know everything about the CFP, their parents' deaths, the stolen money, name changes, everything.

'Brian, I'm so sorry I didn't tell you. She swore me to secrecy, and I didn't know what else to do.'

Brian's voice is soft. He's just grateful that Barbara is talking now, and he's happier than he thought he would be to hear Jane's voice.

'She's your big sister. I get it. The important thing is that we can move forward now, you know?'

'Do they think they can find him; Melvin? Do they believe Kate is alive?'

Brian pauses for a moment. It's difficult to discuss the possible death of his daughter. But, this has given him real hope, and the fact that they believe Kate might be part of the prophecy might keep her safe; the same way Barbara was given certain privileges at the ranch because they wanted her to conceive a child.

'They've got images of him, apparently, and hopefully they will get those circulating. The police are back on this, and giving it their all. They really are. Hopefully they can track him down, and if there's trouble finding him, maybe they can use the media to get the public involved.'

Jane speaks through tears of joy and relief. She has also been living a lie about the past, and her family have no idea what's going on. Now that Barbara has spoken, she's decided to find the courage to tell her ex-husband and kids what happened when she was younger. Before they hang up, Brian says he wants to ask her one question:

'Why did you leave and go back to the States?'

Jane hesitates. She hasn't planned what to say. She never thought she would be in this position.

'I'll be honest with you, honey. I left England again because I thought, well, I figured I might actually be safer the further away from Barbara I was. I was scared they'd come after her again, but they had no interest in me. I was nothing to them, and either were my parents.'

Brian nods to himself.

'That actually makes a lot of sense, Jane. Thanks for telling me. I guess you had your own life to live, and your own healing to do.'

Brian hangs up the phone, and turns to see Lydia behind him, leaning against the doorway. He jumps when he sees her, and she bursts out laughing. But the smile soon vanishes from her face when her father tells her the bad news; Aunt Jane is coming over in a couple days and she's bringing cousin Jenny with her.

44

Lana Nowicki sits in a coffee shop with a laptop in front of her. She's on the phone to McCarthy, and running through all of the files she has on Melvin Todd and the CPF. Some of the information is confidential, and he would ordinarily need special authorisation to access it, but she can go through it with him on the phone. She tells him about the statistics she gathered in the 90s concerning missing people and reports made to police about families suddenly disappearing to join the church, and cutting off all ties with the outside world. The church targeted families, not individuals, that way it was less likely that anyone would report the strange behaviour to the police. Whole families up and moving to a cult might raise a few eyebrows, but if they had recruited individuals, there would have been more of a danger that people would cause trouble for them.

'It wasn't too dissimilar to what we saw at Jonestown or even some of the cults in India. You had a leader, Joseph Todd, and his disciples, the 'elders', all men of course. They sat right at the top of the food chain. At the CFP, these guys were all rapists, and they were definitely responsible for the deaths of multiple people as far as I'm concerned. But, with no witnesses or anyone to identify the remains, we had to drop the case and let them go. Their power was in numbers.'

As Lana is speaking, McCarthy has a disturbing thought; if there was power in numbers, then perhaps there still is. If Melvin Todd is responsible for Kate Stone's disappearance, then he wasn't working alone. He's interrupted by a call that has just come through from another contact in the US. Detective Maclaren signals to him from outside his office that it's important, and he tells Lana he'll have to call her back. He follows DCI Maclaren to her desk in the main office, and she hands him the receiver. He says hello, and listens intently to the young male American voice on the other end.

'Hi there. Detective McCarthy, we ran that ID you wanted us to, and matched it with the photograph you sent too, sir. We believe that this man – Melvin Todd – travelled from Dallas, Texas to London, England two years ago. We believe he's still somewhere in Europe. The flight was one way, and he hasn't used his passport to travel, since.'

McCarthy can hardly believe it.

'Did he travel alone?'

'No sir, he travelled with his spouse, name of Christine Mary Todd.'

45

Lydia opens the fridge and hums to herself as she pulls out a packet of sliced cheese and a small tub of roasted tomatoes.

'Is this hummus still edible?' she shouts back towards Jared's bedroom.

She's only wearing underwear and one of Jared's shirts, and she starts to shiver as she rummages through the cupboards looking for more food.

'This is depressing! We should have ordered takeaway. I'm so hungry!'

She shuffles back to the room with a tray piled with boxes, packets, and jars. Jared smiles at her, and shakes his head from side to side as he pulls back the covers and fixes the pillows so she can get in next to him. Lydia giggles as she starts to put relish and cheese on tiny oatcakes, stopping occasionally to grab a few cashew nuts, and shove them into her mouth. She has been here since early evening and hasn't eaten since noon. She's ravenous.

'Oh my God, sex makes me hungry.'

Jared watches Lydia closely, and when she becomes too self-conscious under his gaze, he turns away for a moment to check his phone.

'Shit. I've got three missed calls from the office. Stay here.'

Jared is on his feet and walking across the room as he waits for someone to pick up at the office. He grabs a robe from the back of the door on the way out and gives Lydia a wink. She sighs to herself as she puts the tray of food down on the floor beside the bed and listens to the sound of his gentle, calm voice drifting towards her from down the hall. Tonight had been the first time they'd had sex, and Lydia was really happy that they had got to know one another and fall in love before they were intimate like that. The relationship was still forbidden because Jared was not allowed to form a relationship with anyone involved with any of the cases he was working on. It wasn't illegal to date Lydia, but it could put his career in jeopardy, and they still had to tread carefully. Lydia hoped that as soon as Kate was home, they could pretend to meet at a party, or at the gym, and tell their friends and family the good news. They were in love and wanted a future together. That was clear now, more than ever. Ten minutes later Jared comes back into the room and his face looks serious.

'You're going to have to go, Lydia.'

His voice is apologetic. Lydia was already planning on staying the night, and telling her dad she was with a friend, so her heart sinks a little at his words.

'I'm going to be working all night, and might have to go into the station. They're planning something. It's to do with Kate, but I can't go into the details.'

Lydia leaps into action and jumps out of the bed.

'You have to tell me. What is it? Have they found her? Oh my God!'

Jared shakes his head. He can't risk blowing this operation.

'This is exactly why we aren't supposed to date one another! I can't tell you, baby, but just believe me that we are doing everything we can to find her, okay? We don't know where she is but we are trying very hard to find out.'

Jared is holding Lydia by the shoulders, and she nods in understanding. She can see that he's doing his best, and suddenly feels guilty about coming here in the middle of all of this. What would her sister think? Jared can see the change in her, and pulls her close, telling her it's all okay, and to call him when she gets home. As soon as she's gone, he picks up the phone again, and tells them he's coming in to help. They're in the midst of setting up a media campaign to find Kate using photographs of Melvin and Christine Todd. Jared needs to be up to speed on everything, and if they need someone to go undercover, he needs to be ready.

46

Melvin has been spending a lot of time with Kate over the past few days. He seems scared that her fever will return, and has even created a medical kit with a blood pressure monitor, thermometer, and stethoscope to be kept next to her bed. He seems reluctant to leave the house too, and has asked Christine to watch her more closely. The couple are not really speaking to one another though, and Kate heard Melvin beating Christine again a couple of nights ago. It seems that his violence peaks when he's stressed, and Kate is aware that any misbehaviour or stress-inducing activity from her might make Christine's life more difficult. She hates being part of this twisted arrangement; stuck in between two people who wouldn't know what respect, love, or kindness were if it hit them in the face. Especially Melvin. Kate can see that he is rotten to the core, and he repulses her more and more as each day goes by. She is still desperately waiting for a moment when she can go downstairs and make that call. Today is Sunday. Up to a few weeks ago, both Melvin and Christine left the house on a Sundays for mass, but lately he has wanted to go alone, for some reason. This could be the perfect opportunity for Kate to go downstairs; she would more than likely be untied, and then all she needed was for Christine to be in a different part of the house, like the kitchen, or even in the garden, and she could open the door using the lamp piece and go downstairs to the phone. So much could go wrong, but it was possible. Kate tries to remain positive and calm; focusing on executing the plan as well as she can. She hears Melvin leave, and pretty soon Christine comes upstairs and goes into the bathroom. Kate calls to her. Christine seems to be in a good mood for some reason, and happily agrees to take her to the bathroom. As she unties her hands, Kate asks if it's okay to stay untied for a while to do a little bit of walking around the room because her back is sore. She doesn't want to make a big deal out of it, and adds that she's happy to wait until Melvin gets home if Christine is busy with housework. Christine doesn't respond right away. Kate can see how incredibly indecisive she is, and thinks that it probably comes from years of living under the wrath of a monster like Melvin. The woman is terrified of making a mistake, and Kate telling her she has a sore back is probably making her worry if she doesn't let her move around, she might get worse, and Melvin might blame Christine. But, she has to prepare the Sunday lunch, and he's also told her to have the kitchen spotless by the time he gets back. Kate couldn't have hoped for a better outcome, and her suggestion works perfectly. Christine walks her back to the room from the bathroom, and tells her she will be up to check on her in fifteen minutes, then locks the door behind her. Kate immediately moves to action. She takes a few deep breaths, then creeps to the door, listening for any evidence that Christine is nearby. All she can hear is the distant mooing of cows, and the birds chirping outside the window. She has already considered the window as a way to escape, but it would mean smashing it because it didn't open, and had been sealed thoroughly. Plus, Kate couldn't risk jumping from the first floor, even if she did manage to smash the glass and climb on to the ledge. She couldn't risk hurting the baby. It's a bright winter's day, and she wishes she could just open the bedroom door, run downstairs, and into the garden. But, she has to stay calm, and not take any more risks than she needs to. She just has to make that call. Then, a thought occurs to her; if Christine catches her this time, what will she do? Will she stay silent, like before? Will there be a physical struggle? Is Kate capable of taking Christine on physically if she has to? Maybe, she should try to sneak up on her, and hit her over the head with something; that's the kind of thing you would see in a movie. The thought makes Kate's heart race, and her feet feel wobbly. Plus, if it backfires, she would be putting her life, and her baby's life in further danger. She decides to stick to the plan of trying to get to the phone.

When she feels that the coast is clear and Christine is down in the kitchen, Kate slowly unlocks the door, opens it, and peeks outside. She can hear her heart beating hard in her ears, until it seems to block out all other sounds. She takes a deep breath, and tiptoes down the stairs, stopping at the bottom. She sees that the door at the end of the hall, leading to the kitchen is ajar. Inside, she can hear Christine chopping vegetables, and the radio is on, too. The sound is alien to Kate. She hasn't heard a radio in so long, and the strangers' voices seem to call out to her, and offer strength. They are the first voices she has heard besides Melvin's and Christine's in forever, and are a welcome reminder of the life and freedom that exists outside of this house. She doesn't waste any time and quickly walks over to the shelf and finds the key. She tries to stop her hands from shaking as she puts it in the lock. It fits! A rush of adrenaline courses through her as she unlocks the phone and lifts the receiver to her ear.

47

Lydia and Brian have just come home after a long morning meeting at the station. The police now have a media team who are dealing with the campaign to find Melvin Todd and his wife, with the hope of finding Kate too, and nationwide support units are ready to strike if a member of the public calls in with information. The campaign is hours away from kicking off, and soon the images of Melvin and Christine will be on every television screen in the country.

Brian is silent, and walks slowly up and down the kitchen, tapping the table gently as he passes it, over and over. Both he and Lydia know the enormity of what's happening; if someone recognises Melvin and Christine Todd from the photographs, it could mean they might know where Kate is, very soon. But it's a dangerous operation. If the Todds see their images on television, and know the police are looking for them, they could do something drastic, and it might make Kate's situation worse, assuming she's still alive.

'Dad, you should try to get some sleep. I know you didn't sleep a wink last night. Have an hour's nap. Nothing is going to happen for a while, anyway.'

Lydia didn't sleep last night either, but the least she can do is pretend that everything is going to be okay.

'You want one of my sleeping pills?'

Brian smiles weakly, and shakes his head.

'I'll see you in an hour, sweetheart. I'll go and have a lie-down. You were so brave today, by the way. I don't know what I'd do without you.'

Lydia smiles back at her father; their relationship has changed so much in the past seven months. On her nineteenth birthday in August, it had seemed like she had gained a decade. Her father seemed more like an equal and a friend than anything else. Kate's disappearance, and then her mother's breakdown had meant they had to become a team, just the two of them, and had to be honest and open with one another. Lydia felt guilty for not telling her dad about Jared. In fact, if it had been up to her, she would have shared it with him, but Jared was adamant that if anyone found out, he would be in serious trouble, and at the very least, be taken off Kate's case entirely.

Lydia walks to the sofa, and curls up next to Molly, who is sleeping soundly on one of the large navy-blue cushions. She texts Jared quickly, and then strokes Molly's head; the dog opens one eye, and sighs happily at seeing Lydia so close. Lydia is filled with emotion all of a sudden. What she wouldn't give to have her sister here with her, right now. Then, Lydia is flooded with warmth, and as if Molly senses the shift too, she opens both of her eyes, lifts her head and looks around at the open door. Hairs stand up on Lydia's neck. She can sense her sister's presence. She almost falls off the sofa when she hears the telephone ringing in the hall. Molly is up, barking, and running towards the phone, and Lydia's first thought is that it's the hospital, and something has happened to her mother, then she thinks maybe the police need them to come in again or have found some new information. She gets to the phone on the fourth ring, and can hear the door to her parents' bedroom creaking open; her dad must have heard it too. Kate's voice greets Lydia as soon as she says 'Hello'. Lydia clutches the receiver with both hands, and presses it to her ear. This moment is something she had imagined so many times. She gasps in shock and disbelief at what she's hearing. The phone suddenly becomes a precious, fragile thing, and Lydia's whole world shrinks down to the size of it. She wants to climb inside, and pull her sister out.

'Kate? Kate! Oh my God. Where are you?'

Tears stream down Lydia's face, and she bends over double in disbelief, and strains to hear her sister's response. Kate's voice is calm, and much quieter than hers.

'I don't know where I am, but the people who kidnapped me, call themselves Melvin and Christine, and they're American. They are part of some sick cult. And... I'm pregnant Lydia.'

Lydia is trying to take it all in, but her mind is racing. She doesn't know what to do. Her dad is next to her now, and trying to grab the phone. Lydia pushes him away.

'Can you leave? How can we find you?'

'I don't know, Lydia. Can you trace this call? I assume the police can trace it, and come find me. Tell them there are two dogs here, and I'm on the first floor, the bedroom with the blue door, we're in the countryside, near farms and things...'

Brian grabs the phone.

'Kate?'

'Dad!'

'Darling! Oh, my darling girl! Where are you? We love you and we miss you so much. Oh God, Kate.'

Kate is keeping an eye on the open door leading to the kitchen, and can see Christine's reflection on a glass-fronted painting in there. She's coming. Kate quickly tells her dad she's got to go, puts the phone down, turns, and runs to the stairs. She takes them two at a time, and just as she gets to the top landing, she turns to see Christine staring at her from below; her face twisted in rage. She puts one foot on the first step, and grabs the bannister, glaring at Kate, she shouts:

'What are you doing?'

By the last syllable she's almost screaming, and her face is bright red with anger. Kate doesn't have a plan; she can't blame fever this time. It's obvious she's trying to escape.

'I... I... please... I just wanted to see what you were doing and I thought...'

Christine isn't buying it, and she shakes her head furiously, muttering something to herself, then, turns around and surveys the hall and front door. She is trying to figure out if Kate was close to escaping. What would she tell Melvin when he got home? He was going to hit the roof. Kate winces as Christine's eyes land on the phone. She didn't have time to put the lock back on, and the key was on the table next to it. It was obvious what she'd done.

'Please, don't tell him! I didn't do anything I swear! I don't want to upset anyone. I just wanted to hear my sister's voice, okay!?'

Kate can't hold it in anymore. She falls to her knees and starts to sob uncontrollably. Hearing Lydia and her dad made everything seem more unbearable for some reason. The parts of her heart that she had to harden since being here were thawed out now she had the chance to speak to the people she loved. Suddenly, Kate is aware that Christine is talking to someone. Melvin must've come back for some reason. Could he know what had happened? Kate slowly gets to her feet as Christine walks out of sight and towards the front door. Kate looks towards Melvin and Christine's bedroom; her mind racing with thoughts of trying to escape. This could be the end for her. If Christine tells

Melvin what she did, there's no way they will ever trust her again. Who knows what he might do to her, and the baby. She finds herself walking into their bedroom. The air is dead and musty in here, and there's a faint smell of stale alcohol, and something like menthol. The curtains are drawn, but there's enough light for Kate to see books on the shelf, and some photographs of Melvin and his family or fellow church members. She doesn't know what she's looking for exactly, but she pulls the curtain back, and finds a locked window. She tries it a few times and looks around for the key. Downstairs, she can hear Melvin's raised voice, and Christine's pleas. She needs to think fast; she needs a weapon to be able to defend herself against him. She will not end up like that other girl. Kate opens the top drawer of the dresser by the window, and within seconds, her hand discovers it; a knife wrapped in a heavy, blue leather case. She feels like she was meant to find it, and without hesitating takes it, leaving the case, and runs back to her bedroom, closing the door behind her. Then, she takes the piece of metal from her pocket and starts to turn the large safety lock on the door so it looks like she never left the room. She can hear shuffling downstairs now, and Christine shrieking; he must have guessed what happened and seen the phone. Kate tries to stay calm, wraps the knife in a hoody, pushes it under her pillow, gets into bed, and picks up the bible from her bedside table. She can pretend to be reading that.

Kate lies in bed for the next half an hour; listens to the arguing below, and hears a loud thump, and then another. Like something is being banged against the wall. Then, footsteps on the stairs.

While Kate was about to sneak downstairs, Melvin had popped into a hardware store to pick up some glue to fix a cupboard handle in the kitchen. That's when he saw his photograph on the television behind the counter, felt the blood drain from his head, and his heart begin to race. He watched as photographs of he and Christine filled the screen. His hand went to his mouth as he tried to figure out how anyone could know it was him; they had been so careful with their movements, and always used false names when they were outside. The house, car, or phone line wasn't in their names, either, and they didn't have any friends who weren't church members. Then, his thoughts went to Barbara Stone. Maybe she had guessed it. Would the police have listened to her after all these years? Surely, they would need some proof before doing something as drastic as this? The news piece showed a photograph of Kate sitting on a garden swing, underneath were images of Melvin and Christine with 'WANTED' in large red letters, and a telephone number to call with information. Melvin's face had gone bright red, he dropped the glue on the counter, and shouted goodbye to the shop worker at the back of the store who was helping another customer with some tins of paint. He knew he couldn't stay in Southam. It was too dangerous now; anyone in the village could be watching this, and the police could be on their way. He needed some advice. He needed to make a call.

By the time he got to the front door at the farmhouse, he already knew what he had to do.

Jared arrives at the Latters' cottage in Banbury, Oxfordshire at around 11.45AM. Someone needed to let them know that the people they believed kidnapped Kate Stone may be connected to Melanie. He couldn't tell them about Ida's visions and the fact that they drew Lydia and him to make the connection in the first place, but he could prepare them in case they discovered something about their daughter, or were approached by members of the public who knew something after seeing the news today.

Jared has been at their home before. A few days after Melanie went missing back in 2015, he had been asked to help out on the case, and went to interview the family, as well as a few friends of Melanie's. Just six weeks previous to that, he had tracked two missing girls down at a drug den in Coventry, and at the time there was every chance Melanie had been trafficked in the same way. He needed to be there to spot any possible connection. Nobody seemed to be able to offer any explanation about where she might be back then, but her family did say that she'd been much quieter in herself before the night she went missing. Jared had wanted to know if she might have had any friends or boyfriends that they didn't know about; that was usually the case with situations like this; girls fall for an older guy, get groomed, and isolated from their friends and family. Melanie sounded like someone who might be targeted. She was beautiful, but not popular, and her mother said that she liked spending time on her own much more than her siblings.

Today, Jared feels the same familiar pang of guilt and empathy when Annie opens the door as he did in

2015. He feels like he had failed her then; given hope, then disappeared. Now, he sees a broken woman before him. Annie's large, sunken eyes are darker and emptier than he remembers, and the light in them has almost gone out. He has seen too many heartbroken mothers in this line of work, and it only fuels him to keep on trying to save as many victims as he can. But, now Jared thinks Melanie wasn't sex-trafficked at all. If their theory is proved right, it seems like she was caught up in a twisted, deluded fantasy that was spawned from the mind of a mad man. Before Kate had been taken, Melvin had more than likely lost patience and decided to take another girl that looked like her, instead. Or maybe he was practising his kidnapping skills, and wanted to see how it felt to overpower someone else, before he got his disgusting hands on Kate.

'Mrs Latter... I need to let you know that we are looking for a man and woman at the moment, in connection with another missing girl: Kate Stone. I wanted to show you their photographs in case you recognise them. There's no evidence whatsoever that they are connected to your daughter, but we thought it was worth checking.'

Annie nods in response and seems eager to see the photographs.

'Please. Of course. Show me. I know Kate Stone, well I know about her and I met her parents once at this special London event about missing people. I always thought that she and Melanie could be sisters.'

Jared nods at her in understanding.

'There is a definite likeness. I would have to agree with you there.'

Jared can see that Annie is getting anxious; her

hands are shaking. He takes the paper folder containing the photographs of Melvin and Christine Todd from his briefcase, and gently places them on the table in front of her. Annie stares hard at the images, picks them up, and scrutinizes their faces.

'Who are these people?'

Jared isn't sure how much he can tell her. He clears his throat, and awkwardly adjusts his watch.

'I can't say much I'm afraid, but we have reason to believe that they wanted to harm the Stone family in some way. I'm sorry I can't tell you anything more right now, Mrs Latter.'

Annie accepts his explanation. She nods to herself. Her glazed-over eyes stare at the carpet.

'You think they might have mistaken Melanie for Kate Stone? Or taken girls that look like that? Do you think Kate is alive, Mr Cooper? Could my daughter be alive too?

Annie is suddenly animated, and her face looks pained. Her eyes fill with fresh tears, and Jared can see that they are tears of hope. He feels like he has failed again; offering a lifeline, and then failing to deliver anything at all.

'Mrs Latter. Please. We don't know anything yet, or even if we're able to track these people down. But, we're hoping that now that we have started to show their photographs on TV, someone, somewhere will recognise them. Then, we feel like we might be a step closer to getting the answers we need.'

Jared wants to get out of there. He hands Annie his number and tells her to call him if she needs anything. He doesn't want to get her hopes up too much. At the back of his mind he knows that the best they can hope to offer the Latters is the chance to bury their daughter when they find her body.

'Thank you for seeing me today. I just wanted you to be aware of this. Please stay in touch, Mrs Latter.'

Annie smiles weakly as she shuts the door behind Jared. Inside, she sits on a chair in the hallway and stares at a photograph of her daughter on the shelf across from her. A wave of pain washes over her body, moving from her feet up through her legs, abdomen, chest, shoulders. It travels down the length of her skinny arms, and into her cold, dry hands, then it seems to gather in the pit of her stomach like a heavy bowling ball. She felt sure she would never feel joy again; never feel the lightness or beauty of life. Without Melanie, she was a shell, and all she could do was go on as best she could, trying to be there for her husband and her two other children. But, what if this Jared Cooper was right, and Kate Stone was connected to Melanie's disappearance? What if they were together somewhere? She could feel the hope, like a tiny butterfly, just leaving its cocoon, trying to gain strength. Could she let herself feel it? Was it possible that her daughter was still out there somewhere, after all this time?

Back in the car, Jared checks his phone, and sees two missed calls from the London office, and fifteen from Lydia, as well as a text from her begging him to call as soon as possible. Without thinking, he makes the decision to call her first, and she picks up almost immediately; her voice is loud and excited; it sounds like she's running and out of breath.

'Jared. She's alive! Oh my God, Kate's alive...'
Lydia bursts into tears.
'Slow down. Slow down. What do you mean?'

'She called us… said she was pregnant, Jared, and in the countryside. She said the people who had her were called Melvin and Christine. It's definitely them and they have her!'

Jared's face drops in shock at Lydia's words.

'You… you called the station?'

'Yes! The police are tracking the call right now! We're on our way to the station. I'm going inside. Come!'

Brian tugs at his daughter's sleeve, and tells her to hang up the phone as they enter the station. He wonders why she has called Jared Cooper, and looks at her quizzically. But Lydia's on a different planet, and barely feels his hand tugging at her or notices that he's listening to the call in the first place.

'I love you. I love you! See you soon.'

Lydia hangs up, and then turns to see her father staring at her.

'What the hell was that? Who do you love?'

Lydia smiles, then laughs and points at him.

'Your face! I'll tell you later, Dad.'

McCarthy meets them at the front desk, and asks them to follow him to his office.

50

Kate braces herself as she hears the key in the door. This is it. Melvin comes into the room much more calmly than she expected him to.

'I'm sorry you had to hear us arguing just now. Christine was supposed to be doing something, and once again, she has ignored my wishes and... never mind. I don't want to bore you with the details.'

Melvin smiles, almost shyly, in Kate's direction. He has never acted like this before. He looks at her like she's a stranger.

'How are you feeling, Kate?' he suddenly asks.

'How far along do we think you are again with the baby? Is it nearly six months now, or more? Not long to wait, huh? I mean, some babies are actually born after that length of time, and they survive, don't they?'

Kate is unsure what Melvin is trying to get at, but instinct tells her that he is having some very deluded thoughts.

'No. That's very rare. I mean, sometimes in hospital, babies can survive if they are premature but it's extremely dangerous.'

She laughs nervously and adjusts the covers over her belly.

'It could be another ten weeks, or longer, before this baby is ready to be born.'

At hearing this, Melvin looks distressed. He has suddenly started to sweat, and mutters something to himself, then swears loudly. Kate is pretty sure the is having some sort of psychotic episode; his eyes are almost black, and he keeps on opening his mouth and showing his teeth. He loosens his shirt collar as if he's having trouble breathing. Kate has to tread carefully now, and still doesn't know if he is aware that she went downstairs and used the phone. But there is a chance that Christine took the blame, or covered for her in some way. She has to stay on his good side to stay safe.

'Melvin, are you alright? Do you need some water? Or a rest maybe?'

He turns and glares at her.

'Don't you tell me what I need! You're causing me so much trouble right now! You have no idea!'

His nostrils flare and his whole face burns red. He looks like he's about to keel over and go in cardiac arrest, and Kate wishes with every bone in her body that he would. If there is a God, surely, he will act now, and get rid of this pathetic monster from the planet. Her mind wanders. Maybe the police are already on their way. They could have traced the call by now. Maybe she will be with her family tonight, and the nightmare will finally be over. Melvin is staring at her again.

'You think I'm stupid, don't you? You think I don't know what I'm doing.'

Kate is dumbstruck.

'What do you mean? No, no. I don't think that at all.'

Melvin snarls at her. His face is contorted. He doesn't look like himself.

'Get up! Get up now, before I make you, stupid bitch!'

Kate cowers in the bed. He comes closer, pulls the covers from her, and she moves one hand behind her back to feel the knife handle pressing hard against her fingers.

51

McCarthy and Davies are on the M1 headed out of London. It's been four hours since Kate made the call to her father and sister. It seemed to take forever for the trace to be complete, and when they finally got an address, it made more sense for them to engage the help of the Banbury police. They could at least get some men on the ground to assess the situation and report anything unusual, as well as secure the spot so no-one could get in or out. It's going to take at least another forty minutes for McCarthy and Davies to reach the location, even at this speed, and every minute that goes by means that Kate is in more danger. If it wasn't for the fact that they ran Melvin and Christine's photographs on the news today, McCarthy would have wanted to get there himself before doing anything, but he couldn't risk the wait now. If Melvin knows they're on to him, he'll be on guard, and more vigilant than ever.

Eventually, the Banbury team arrive at the location and begin to assess it, letting McCarthy know about the security gate, dogs, and truck inside.

'There's a light on upstairs in the house that corresponds to the room the girl spoke about during the phone call, sir. There is a security light at the gate that's come on, but there's no obvious way to get past it without drawing attention to ourselves.'

'Scale the wall for God's sake.'

McCarthy barks down the phone, then changes his mind, almost immediately.

'Look, we are less than half an hour away. Maybe you should wait. Just wait, alright. Back off.'

The siren blasts out loudly through the darkening

country roads, and they're going over ninety miles an hour. Davies has never seen his partner so agitated. Twenty-two minutes later, they approach the long, bumpy driveway to the farmhouse, and McCarthy slows right down, instructing Davies to call the officers back to let them know that they're approaching. They drive past the woods towards the main gate where the officers are waiting, and McCarthy gets nervous, very nervous. Kate was alive this morning, and it's up to him to make sure that she stays alive. These next moves are the most important; the Todds could turn violent with her if they feel under threat. Davies stops, and turns the car lights off about twenty metres from the gate. McCarthy gets out, quickly walks towards the group, and orders everyone to stay silent and keep all lights off, except for the small torch that he and Davies will take with them. It's not even five o'clock but already dark.

'I'm going over this.' he tells Davies quietly as he assesses the ten-foot wall, either side of the security gate.

'…and you're coming.'

Davies thinks he can see that the wall ends about thirty metres from where they're standing.

'Should we not try to go through the line of trees, and get in round the back, boss?'

McCarthy scolds himself for not exploring that option, and starts to walk towards the line of trees without saying a word to Davies, who follows him diligently, waving and shrugging to the other officers. But, the wall continues behind the trees and McCarthy swears at Davies for making him look like an idiot. His patience is wearing thin.

'Let's just get over this thing, yeah?'

Davies offers to give McCarthy a leg up, and when McCarthy's on top of the wall, he starts to scramble up himself.

'Not so hard, is it?' McCarthy whispers.

This was it. This is a moment he never thought they would get to; having an actual location that Kate Stone was at. The past nine months flash through McCarthy's mind from that first day he heard that Kate was missing. He thinks about Haven and the strange masked man that they saw on CCTV footage. This was one of the biggest and strangest cases he had ever worked on, and now he needs to make sure he doesn't mess it up at the last hurdle. He needs to get Kate out of there alive.

He and Davies jump from the wall, and land on the damp grass at the same time, then slowly make their way to the back of the house. They peek in the windows; every curtain and blind is open, and every room looks empty, or nearly empty. McCarthy can hear the dogs barking at the front gate. He radios the officers, and tells them to move further down the wall to see if the dogs will move down that way too, and away from discovering McCarthy and Davies. The less noise near the house, the better. It works, and the barking becomes more distant and sporadic.

'It actually helps to keep them occupied down there, eh?' Davies whispers.

McCarthy is walking slowly around the side of the house.

'Right, I want you to knock on the door at the front. I'll stay around here because I've got a view of the inside. That will give us the advantage, if and when one of them answers.'

Davies looks terrified, and McCarthy gives him a stern look.

'Do it. We're good to go. Don't let me down, Davies.'

Davies nods at his partner, looks away for a moment, then back to him again. He trusts McCarthy more than anyone he knows, and he doesn't want to do anything wrong here. He wants to prove that he's a good detective and can keep his cool. McCarthy, sensing what's going through his head, gives him a firm pat on the shoulder, then pushes him gently towards the front of the house. McCarthy waits by the window at the side of the house, and keeps an eye on the hallway inside, leading to the front door. Davies pushes the doorbell, and the sound rings out loudly throughout the house.

Jared answers Lydia's call on the fourth or fifth ring.

'Where the hell have you been? I've called you about twenty times in the past hour.'

Lydia doesn't even wait for him to answer, and immediately announces that she and her dad are on the way to Northamptonshire.

'They haven't given us the exact address, Jared. Can you help?'

Jared had a feeling this would happen. It's precisely why he didn't pick up the phone earlier.

'There's no way you can go there. It's too risky, Lydia. You know that. The police will know exactly what to do, and having anyone else around could ruin things. It could put Kate in even more danger.'

Lydia's heart sinks. She knows he's right.

'Okay. Okay. We know that. We do. But we want to be nearby, in case... when they find her, we want to be there for her, Jared.'

'Look, why don't you both just go get a coffee somewhere and I can meet you later? That sound good? There's a little village called Southam. Put it into your GPS. Let me know when you're there, and I'll drive to you, okay?'

Lydia is already typing the destination into the navigation system in the car, and can see that they'll be there in less than thirty minutes.

'Half an hour, okay? Please tell me as soon as you hear anything.'

'Okay, Lydia. See you soon. Careful on the road.'

Brian is staring, wide-eyed at the dark road ahead. He hasn't said anything for the last twenty minutes, and is just concentrating on getting close to Kate, as quickly and safely as possible. But he can't ignore what he's just heard.

'What's going on with you and this man, Lydia? How old is he?'

Lydia hasn't really planned what to say about the relationship. It was an accident that she had said 'I love you' on the phone to Jared earlier. She had just been so excited about the call from Kate that she wasn't thinking. How could she deny everything now?

'Dad, I'm so sorry that I didn't tell you. I wanted to, and I'm glad you know, now. But Jared would get into so much trouble at work if anyone found out about us. Dad, we're in love. He's amazing, and he makes me so happy.'

Brian interrupts her, and without even glancing in her direction, he angrily asks again, how old Jared is.

'He's not that old Dad. He's just turned thirty. He's so much better to me than Simon was, and he listens to me.'

Lydia can see that her father's having a hard time digesting the information he's just heard. She decides to give him a moment to take it in, and looks out the window, instead. A light drizzle covers the car in tiny zigzags of rainwater, and Lydia traces one with her finger on the inside of the passenger window. Her mind goes to her sister. For all they know, they might have found her already. She tries to imagine what it will be like to see her, and hug her again. She'd said she was pregnant. Kate was going to have a baby! Lydia was going to be an aunt, their parents were going to be grandparents! Lydia can feel the conflict of emotions warring inside of her; the joy and expectation of Kate being returned safely, and the nightmare finally being over, and the opposite; a fear that she will never be the same, and the horror of what happened to her while she was with this evil man damaging her forever. Lydia reminds herself that she has to be strong, and feels a pang of guilt for causing her dad to worry about her and for lying to him about Jared. She was supposed to be mature and dependable, and had told him to treat her like an adult and confide in her, but she hadn't afforded him the same respect.

'Dad?'

Her voice is soft, childlike, and she clears her throat to try to make it stronger.

'Dad?' she proffers again.

Brian stops the car at traffic lights, and indicates left. He glances at the GPS screen first, then looks at his daughter. His face softens.

'We're going to be alright, Lyds. Don't worry about this Jared thing. I get it. Your secret is safe with me, and… I won't tell anyone. I get it.'

Lydia smiles appreciatively at him, and nods her head at his words, but before she can respond, the phone rings on her lap.

'Shit. It's Mum. What should I say?'

'Don't answer, darling.'

Lydia scrunches her nose in discomfort at the incoming call, and thinks about her mother, worrying in the hospital bed.

'You're right. It might be too much for her, and she'll feel awful that she's not with us. Okay. I won't answer.'

A few minutes later, Lydia listens to Barbara's voicemail. She sounds confused and emotional. Her voice is almost a whisper.

'Lydia, p-please… I need someone… anyone to talk to me, and listen. Oh… I've had the most awful, terrifying dream. I dreamed that someone was trying to rescue your sister. They came close to getting to her and then... oh... then there was an awful struggle and blood and screams... please call me, darling. I love you.'

Lydia's whole body feels hard and cold at hearing her mother's message. She tries to shake it off, but as they pull into the carpark at the pub in Southam, she feels scared. The reality of the situation hits her, and she turns to her dad. He's already thinking the same thing; what if it all goes terribly wrong?

When no-one comes to the door, McCarthy tells the men outside to climb the wall and join them. A few minutes later, two armed officers follow McCarthy's instructions, and break the side window so they can enter the house. Two other officers take the dogs outside now that they can open the security gate, and McCarthy and Davies wait outside, as the men clear the first room and make their way down the hallway. One of the officers continually announces that police are entering the home and are looking for Melvin and Christine Todd. In less than five minutes, McCarthy hears them say something that he has dreaded hearing all day:

'We have blood, lots of blood in here.'

McCarthy climbs through the window with ease. Davies follows closely behind. The officers have turned the lights on, and when McCarthy gets there, he sees blood smeared all over the floor. It looks there was a struggle, or whoever was bleeding was moved. One of the officers looks at McCarthy and then points around the corner.

'We have a body.'

Jared and Brian shake hands. Lydia isn't sure how to act with him in front of her dad, but luckily, Brian excuses himself and goes to the toilets, so that Lydia can hug him without feeling self-conscious. It feels so good to have him there, but the public display of affection makes Jared feel incredibly uncomfortable, and his voice is stern and cold.

'Lydia, your dad could see us! Please.'

Lydia lets go of him, moves away, and smiles, first at Jared, and then to herself, as she sits down at the bright window seat. She can't tell him that her dad knows about them already. Not yet anyway. But soon everything will be out in the open, her sister will be home, Melvin and Christine will be in prison, and everything will be back to normal. Jared is looking at the screen on his phone.

'Have you heard anything?' Lydia asks.

He shakes his head in response.

'Nothing for the past hour now.'

'It's so hard not knowing. Dad and I are going crazy. Is there anything you can tell us?'

Jared smiles at her, checks that Brian isn't already on his way back to the table, then reaches over to squeeze her hand gently, just for a second. A waiter comes, takes their drinks order, and offers to turn the gas fire on. Lydia hadn't even noticed how cold it was until he mentioned the fire, and Jared quietly scolds her for not having a warm coat on. Brian joins them as the tea and coffees arrive, and manages to pour himself a cup of tea, although his hands are shaking. Jared shuffles uncomfortably in his chair, dreading what Brian is going to say next. He's probably wondering what Jared is doing there, and why Lydia called him from the car. Jared's face flushes red, but Brian's tone is warm and genuine.

'It's very nice of you to come to meet us. It's a real comfort to have a professional here I think...to let us know what's going on, and so forth.'

Lydia can see that her father is making effort to make Jared feel at ease, and loves him for it. But, before they can continue, Jared's phone rings.

'Please, excuse me. It's the office. I told them to call as soon as anything happened. They might know something now.'

Jared's on his feet. Outside, he paces the gravelled path, and listens intently. All Brian and Lydia can do is watch him through the window, as he nods down the phone.

'Dad... his face... he doesn't look happy, does he?'

Jared hangs up, and curses to himself, then turns to see Lydia and Brian's desperate faces at the window about ten feet away.

55

McCarthy rounds the corner at the end of the hall, and sees where all the blood has come from. He walks slowly towards the person lying face down on the floor, and can see by the clothing that she's a female. Then, he sees blonde hair. It's not Kate.

'Jesus Christ. It's Christine Todd. Christine, can you hear me?

He kneels next to her, and feels her face. She's warm. Her entire head is covered in blood, and she's unconscious.

'Davies, call the paramedics immediately. She's alive.'

Two other officers have joined them, and are searching the upstairs. McCarthy decides to follow them, and instructs Davies to stay with Christine until the paramedics arrive. The place is empty. McCarthy scans one of the bedrooms, and can see that this was where Kate was kept. He sees the baby books and prayer books, the chains on the bed. Davies joins him a few minutes later and lets him know that the basement is clear too.

'Do you think they saw the news before anyone got the chance to report them?'

'That's exactly what's happened, mate.'

McCarthy is devastated. This is almost the worst-case scenario. If they hadn't run the story and those photographs today, they could have traced Kate from the phone call, and this could all be over. The timing is ridiculously bad. And now, he had to tell the Stones that he had failed them, and the one chance they had of getting their daughter back was ruined. He tries to stay calm, and asks Davies to wait for him downstairs. He needs to gather his thoughts, and sits on the same bed that just hours ago, Kate lay on, terrified about what was going to happen to her. He picks up one of the prenatal care books on the bedside table, and opens it at the bookmark. It's a chapter entitled 'The Third Trimester: Weeks 28 – 40', and McCarthy wonders if this is an accurate indication of how far along in the pregnancy she is. The longer she's carrying the baby, the better. If they can get to her before she gives birth they can make sure she's safe, and the baby too. He calls the office in London and fills them in, telling them to get a forensic team here as fast as possible. They need to go through the entire place for clues about where Melvin and Kate might have gone, and he needs results from the phone line here, in case any calls had been made or received that could indicate where they are.

'Oh, and I'll speak to the family, okay? I believe they're nearby, so I'll go and meet them as soon as I can.'

Downstairs, Davies watches as Christine Todd is carried out on a stretcher and rolled into an ambulance. He struggles to understand what the paramedics are saying, but passes on the message to them that Christine is wanted by police and lets them know what happens when she gets to the hospital. Christine might know where Kate and Melvin are; she is their only hope right now, and she has to remain in custody.

56

Lydia and Brian wait in the garden of the farmhouse for the forensic team to finish. It's dark and cold. They are silent, and have been for nearly an hour. Jared has brought them some blankets and tea, and asks if they want anything to eat, but they both shake their heads and continue to stare at the house in silence. They want to see inside, and won't leave until they do. Lydia doesn't even feel shocked anymore. She feels empty. This is powerlessness and disappointment taken to a new level. They had come so close to Kate, and now this. Why? Why couldn't they have waited one more day before running the photographs of Melvin and Christine, she thinks. They had been told by McCarthy that Christine was in a critical condition, and had more than likely been left for dead, but there was still a chance she could help them to find Melvin and Kate, assuming she makes it.

A few minutes after ten, McCarthy appears and lets them know that the forensic team are finished gathering evidence, and if they still want to look inside the house, he can take them inside.

'But please, don't touch or move anything. Promise me? There could still be valuable evidence inside, and we don't want to compromise that.'

His voice is gentle, as it always is when he speaks to the Stones, but Lydia can see that the day has taken its toll on him, too. He guides Brian and Lydia through the front door, and tells them that the area at the end, where Christine was found, is cordoned off.

'Do you want to take a look upstairs? We are pretty sure Kate's bedroom was up there.'

Brian nods for the both of them, and they make

their way up. Every step, Lydia thinks about the strangeness of the fact that her sister was right here just hours ago. She crept down these stairs to make the phone call just this morning, and crept back up again afterwards, hoping they would trace the call, and come to find her. They enter the bedroom in silence. It's bare, and looks nothing like any space that Kate has lived in before; her room at home is huge, and filled with clothes, shoes, and photographs. This is a cold, silent room, and Lydia walks around it slowly, trying to imagine what her sister did here for all these months. She looks at the bed, and is at least comforted by the fact that there are lots of clean blankets on it; it's not as awful as it could be. She traces her fingers along the material, as if it will somehow bring her closer to her twin. Then, she sees the chains, and looks at McCarthy, questioningly.

'Yes, they're being tested for her DNA, but it looks like she was chained up here.'

Lydia turns away from him, and her eyes land on the small pile of books on the bedside table. They are all pregnancy books, and Lydia thinks again, about the life that's growing inside of her sister.

'She'll be okay, won't she? I mean, this is good, isn't it; the fact that she's pregnant with his child? I mean... he can't hurt her now, can he?'

Brian puts his hand on Lydia's shoulder, and tries to reassure her. He can hear by the tone of her voice that she's struggling to come to terms with all of this.

'Sweetheart, they are doing everything they can to make sure they can still find her, okay? Isn't that right, Detective?'

McCarthy nods confidently.

'Yes. From what we know, the fact that Kate is more

than likely carrying Melvin Todd's child means that he will want her to be safe and healthy. We're doing everything we can to find out where they have gone Lydia. Everything.'

Brian moves towards the door and says he wants to leave. Lydia is actually relieved; she can't stand being here anymore, either.

'I'll let you know where we end up, but I think we'll stay here tonight, in a hotel nearby, in case there's any news.'

McCarthy nods, then shows them downstairs, and out of the house.

'You've got my number, so please use it – anytime – I'll let you know as soon as we know anything.'

Brian and Lydia see Jared waiting outside. He offers to travel with them to a hotel, but Brian shakes his head, and mutters a 'no thanks'. Lydia squeezes his arm, and tells him she'll call as soon as she can, before following her dad to the car.

'Should we call Mum when we get to the hotel?'

Silence.

'Dad?'

Brian shakes his head.

'Sorry, I, I can't think straight right now. Just need to get out of here.'

Lydia understands. The house had been so haunting and strange. Its smells, the chains on the bed, the strange wallpaper... it was like something out of a horror movie. Brian drives without really knowing where he's going. He eventually sees a sign for a hotel called Fawsley Hall☐☐☐☐☐☐☐☐☐☐☐, and turns down the long driveway towards the entrance gates. Lydia notices how isolated and quiet the hotel is. The grounds are extensive, and she can see an old church surrounded by sheep in the distance. If it wasn't for the drawn-out nightmare that they were going through, this would have been exactly the kind of place Lydia would want to come for a relaxing weekend with Jared. Then, another thought enters her head. What if Melvin took Kate somewhere like this? He could easily have got in his car and driven her here, booked a room in the courtyard so that she didn't have to pass through reception. Maybe he had her locked in the boot of his car. Lydia's vivid imagination mixed with paranoia, and this feeling of utter confusion is overwhelming; she can feel her legs growing weak and empty, like all the blood has drained from them.

'Dad, I think I need to get a drink.'

She points at the sign for the hotel bar, and starts to get out of the car before he can even respond.

Just before midnight, the police dogs arrive at the farmhouse. They immediately run to the back of the property, and scratch and bark at the shed-like building at the bottom of the garden. The dog handlers break the lock on the shed door, and let the dogs in. They immediately start to dig at the soil.

'Right, this looks interesting. No flooring and the dogs are on to something...'

McCarthy stands outside praying that it's not Kate. What if Melvin had decided to kill her and the baby, after all? It's not long before the team start digging too, and ten minutes later, the remains of Melanie Latter are uncovered. McCarthy can't believe it. He makes a call to the chief of police, and signs a form to say that the remains can be taken in to be identified. Then, he calls Fran. She's been lying awake, waiting to say goodnight, and can hear the stress in her husband's voice when he speaks to her.

'You're doing a good job, babe. A really good job. Don't be too hard on yourself. You're getting answers.'

McCarthy nods down the phone, but he can barely string a sentence together.

'I've got to go, Fran. I love you, and I love our family.'

He hangs up, and makes a quick plan with Davies about who should tell the Latters when the body is identified.

'There were earrings on that body. Matched the ones Melanie was wearing the night she went missing.'

McCarthy nods at Davies. He had noticed that already.

'Say nothing until the results come back, alright?

Kate sees her reflection in a thin metallic strip that runs down the side of the wardrobe. This morning, the sun had risen, in spite of everything, and now it lights her pale face, showing her, with all of its relentless power and truth, her own reality. There is no escape. The events from the day before are scrambled in Kate's mind. She remembers Melvin coming home and behaving differently. He had told her to follow his instructions carefully, or she and the baby would die. And she believed him. Suddenly, it seemed like he had reached the end of his tether. He told her in a matter-of-fact way, that Christine was dead, and they needed to get out of there. He had said there was a darkness in the house, and if they didn't get away from it, he would end up killing her, the baby, and himself. Miraculously, Kate had managed to stay calm. She tried to reason with him; the whole time thinking that the police were on the way, almost there, if only she could distract Melvin for long enough. She had contemplated pulling the knife from under the pillow behind her and plunging it into his chest, but she had no idea if she had the strength and skill to actually kill him. And what if she just cut him, and enraged him so much that he murdered her? She couldn't take that risk. Not now, anyway. She had walked outside with him without screaming, and got into the boot of his car. They drove for about twenty minutes, until she felt the vehicle slow down and stop. She heard him get out, and then there were other voices. Kate had no idea who these people were. She wondered if she should cry out or scream for help. Maybe they didn't know she was in there. But, instinct told her to stay quiet. Ten minutes after that, the voices went, Melvin opened the boot, told her she was a good girl, and helped her out, and to her feet. They were at the back of a little cottage, and there was an old tractor and some rusty farm equipment next to them. The cottage looked run-down and deserted. Melvin had taken her inside, locked the door, and told her to take a seat, then pulled a scissors from a paper bag, and started to cut her hair. Kate trembled every time he came at her, terrified that he would suddenly stick it into her neck, or decide to cut her throat. His breathing was thick and heavy; sometimes it was almost a groan. Kate guessed that one of the people whose voice she had heard must have given the cottage to him. That meant that they knew about her, probably. There were others in on this whole thing. It wasn't just him and Christine, and some weird prophecy. Then, Melvin took out a box of blonde hair dye, mixed it in a small plastic bowl, and smeared it all over Kate's head. It stank, and he swore at the smell, and the stinging on his hands. She had asked him not to use the dye; afraid that it would harm the baby, and he hit her across the face in response. She had shut up again after that, and stayed silent as they waited ninety minutes for the bleach to strip all of the colour from her hair. Then Melvin had rinsed it off using freezing water in the kitchen sink and washed it with some coconut shampoo he took from the bag.

Now, the smell of bleach and coconut seems to permeate everything. Kate tries to block it out. She stares at herself in the mirrored strip of metal, deep into her dark eyes. She hadn't dared to ask, but she assumes that Melvin was trying to disguise her. And it worked. She couldn't see one bit of the girl she used to be. He had broken her down, and now was rebuilding her.

Kate feels sure that even her voice is different, now. She looks around the room at the mouldy walls, bare mattress, cracked ceiling, the dead insects along the windowsill, the litter on the floor, and the thick layer of dust covering everything. This can't be it. Surely, he didn't expect her to live here with him, to have a baby in this cold, squalid place?

Outside, a crow makes a loud, screeching sound, and for a second, Kate mistakes it for a police siren. She looks at the locked front door, at Melvin pulling some food from a plastic bag, and at the dirty window over the sink. Maybe, if she pretends to be exhausted and goes to sleep, he might not think to tie her up tonight. There are no dogs outside this time, and it would be a lot easier to get out of this place than the farmhouse. She closes her eyes, pictures her parents and Lydia's faces, and promises them that this isn't the end. They will all be together again.

This story continues in the final book in the trilogy: 'This Dark Town III: Us and Them'.

Please leave a review if you enjoyed this book. It is very much appreciated by a self-published author! Thank you!

Printed in Great Britain
by Amazon